Original title,
Published by Free Muskete

SCULPTURE

BEN BOUTER

America Star Books

Author Photo: Marise
Cover Photo: Eric

Softcover 9781632495884
PUBLISHED BY AMERICA STAR BOOKS, LLLP
www.americastarbooks.com

Printed in the United States of America

Acknowledgements

Many Thanks to Eric for meticulously checking all the missing letters and silly mistakes. And of course, to Iris Brown for her countless witty comments and suggestions.

PART 1
FATHER

1

I look down. My father is sitting on the bottom step of the concrete stairs that lead up to my apartment in Troelstrakade. His shiny shoes are firmly rooted on the pavement. A person like him needs to have steady footing. His back is straight as always, like a stick was inserted to make his spine rigid. He wears a gray hat with a carefully placed dent at the center. His gray hair stands out from the indifferent slicing. His dull winter coat is brightened with a green woolen scarf. That was his only indulgence. That was my scarf.

He wears creased pants and a straight face. His thin mouth is concealed by his broad mustache. His suit gives him the illusion that he is a distinguished gentleman largely coveted by women. Just like me, he is absorbed in his own world.

It's minus ten degrees Celsius and freezing. I'm pretty sure that the cold weather will bring some snow. I look at my watch. He must have sat there for about fifteen minutes. A man will naturally have numb buttocks from sitting on the icy concrete. The only thing that insulates him from the cold is the leather soles on his feet. But after some time, the frost climbs up his legs and spreads on his entire body. Even his brains are frozen and his dreams are the only ones that survive

Ben Bouter

I saw him when I came around the corner and suddenly remembered that I had forgotten to do some shopping. He wanted the sickly sweet cake with pink frosting as a snack to compliment his coffee. The cake reminded him of the Japanese flag. He hated those cakes.

I make my way back to the supermarket. I pass by the children who are busy playing in the frozen river in front of my house. They are having fun on the ice. I see a little girl about six years old ahead of me. I see her lagging in her skates instead of the usual smooth glide across the icy surface.

How long has it been since I have last skated?
Have I ever skated?

I yearn to call out the girl's name, walk up to her and put my arm around her as we walk together to the supermarket. Would she shy away from the instant attention?

The trees have all shed their leaves and they are bare in the open cold. Their dreary branches lift up to the sky in anticipation of a fresh, new start. I am lucky that I have my hat and my tights on to keep me warm from the bitter cold. The ice can no longer control me. I am all warm inside.

The Albert Heijn shopping center is nice and cozy. Songs about Santa Claus fill the store. I am amazed that such a popular Christmas personality could convince people to indulge in shopping.
Can't a person be merry without the red suit and white beard illusion?

8

I do not have any memories about Santa Claus. He simply did not exist. We did not believe in such crap and hence, did not receive any gifts during Christmas. Or should I say, we received gifts but certainly not from him. Sometimes it was my mother who gave presents, but she would always give it in secret. She said that gifts spoil a child. I carefully hid my sketch pad and HB pencil. I still keep until now. I was content with my first drawing kit and I happily disappeared in my own world.

I grab the cheapest brand at the coffee section of the supermarket. I am fed up with Max Havelaar and I prefer something else. I unconsciously hum the catchy tunes as I walk around the store. Sometimes the music gets stuck in my head for days and I struggle to delete it from my memory.

I look at the wine bottles on display. There is so much love, so much history in a bottle of red wine. Some vines take forty years to produce the finest grapes. The bottles are aged, while I am not. What did the grapes endure to produce such great taste? Is it the cold weather, heavy snow or heavy rain? The best tasting wine is the most experienced. I cannot resist buying an expensive bottle of wine knowing that the sixty feet long roots are sturdy and resilient. A sip can be comforting and nostalgic. One drink can provide me with immense inspiration.

How do I do it? I look at the real colors and decide if I want to make it dull or brighter. I am still learning how to paint and I love it. Reality is non-existent; it is perspective that survives. I learn through observation. It's crazy how you can transform a man with big ears into a harmonious face with all the right proportions. I fuse in my attitude and my mood determines how I choose the colors. Reality is always disguised. Not everything you see is real. What you read is what you understand. The reader writes his own book, and everyone has a unique story.

I wonder what colors I would use to represent my youth. I am slightly deceived when I reminisce. I had my own world as a child, and it was a realm that adults never thought that it existed. I am now an adult and I have outgrown my childish sphere but I can always look back to it as a wonderful memory.

I walk over to the cashier with the longest queue. I appraise all the customers in front of me while I wait for my turn. At the head of the line is a businessman recently divorced. He picks up the newspaper that serves as his constant companion for an entire year of excessive alimony; a mother with at least three children has filled her cart with a week's supply of groceries, her husband hates shopping and rarely appreciates her efforts, she suspects that her husband is having an affair with an officemate but she does not confront him to keep the fragile peace at home; A little lady who must soon go to a retirement home counts her loose change with hands affected with gout, the same hands she used for her first piano lesson; I stand next to a woman with a wailing child. She has pink streaks in her blond hair. Her jacket has a leopard motif and her fur collar is wide open. Fat people are rarely affected by the cold. Her black lacquered boots end right below her knees.
"Why are you crying? Are you tired?" the woman asked the crying child
"You go ahead, I don't mind," I tell her.
"Thank you! How kind of you." The woman was relieved.
"No problem. You're welcome. What's her name?" I asked.

"His name is Pim," she remarked.

"Oh, I'm sorry. It's hard to tell from that hat." I was embarrassed.

"Is that a girl's hat?" They inspected mine.

"From Nepal!" I wanted to blurt out, but I held my tongue. The child does not budge, it seems like he is frozen in place. I reckon the kid was born and bred in Hoefkade, where only a few kids lived.

"I'm not really good at kids. I don't have one, so it figures," I replied.

She smiles an embarrassed smile while she winks at the woman behind the counter who has flat nest of blond hair on her head. A piece of cotton candy falls on the fat lady's eyelash. Was she Pim's grandmother?

She loaded her groceries on the conveyor in the meantime: sprinkles, coke, a box of beer, and chips line up the register. Her breasts peek from coat as she puts the items on the belt. If they spill out, she'll have to check out Kilo's Top Sellers as well. Then she puts a pack of diapers as her final purchase.

"Are those for you?" I said to myself.

I would have loved to ask the question with a megaphone so the entire store would her answer. I know these guys are as nosy as me.

Pim watches my icing cakes as they make their way to the counter together with the coffee. "Well, this turned out to be another fine day!" she exclaimed after her purchase. I have no idea what she means, but I'm sure that the Holidays bring out the best in all of us. Then she calls out to me and adds: "Tell your father I said hi!" She winks back at the cashier and the blonde woman laughs.

I blush at their comment and quickly pay for the items. They do not know my father like I do.

I was so naïve that I did not realize that the bitch knows me. It's a shame that I have to walk back to the store because Father needs those cakes. Or rather, I need them to please Father. He will eat them tonight together with his sushi.

How long was I out? I check my watch and estimate that I have spent twenty minutes at the store. Twenty five minutes, tops. That gives the people in the store enough time to know my story.

There is a newly opened art gallery around the corner. I see a few people inside but I do not go in. I see exuberant paintings in cobra-like patterns from the gallery's window. I learn from the brochure that the paintings were made by children from India. I stuff the brochure in my bag and retrieve it at a later time. I feel a warm glow as I see the children's artwork.

2

Snow has begun to fall. It is the most magical of all of nature. I find snow very enchanting that it can transform the earth into a fairy tale land in just one night. It's as if the heavens wanted to sanctify the earth and make it pure. Pure white. Snow is just wonderful. The snowflakes float ever so light from the air but it weighs down the branches. It is a mysterious scenario that silently and brutally unfolds right in front of your eyes. The snow and I share mutual fondness for each other. I could spend countless hours by the windowsill and watch as the snowflakes come down by the thousands. I try to trace their paths as they make their way down the house and into the lawn. I consider the snowflakes as my friends, along with Beau and my drawing pad. Oh, and Mom whenever she is around.

Everyone else, especially those in my school, think I am stupid.

The snowflakes fall on the windowsill and I enjoy watching them until they disappear. The flakes always fall together even if they are different. They are family. They fall effortlessly and linger for a moment.

The newly trimmed hedge and the mailbox are now covered with a white blanket and they beckon to me: "Come and get me!"

But I know better. I know a boy who was lured away by the snow. He could still be alive if he did not yield to the enticing snow. But the snow insisted: *Come on, everything is light and fluffy. Snow will not hurt you.* The snow called out to the boy and the boy was the only one who heard its call.

They boy asked me to join him as he rolled the snow into a ball. "Hurry," he said to me. "It will be over in a few days." He rolled the snow until it formed a large and beautiful ball. He kept going and going and when he reached the riverbank, he called out to me to play in the snow.

I walked over to join him. I've seen him around. We went to the same school except he was a few years older than me. He was also a familiar face in the neighborhood; I was certain he lived nearby. I often saw him pass by our window even if he never looked up. He called to me, and from then on I knew we were friends. I think he liked me. For the first time, someone liked me. I ran to him and he was at the edge of the slope. He waved at me and just as I was within arm's reach, he climbed on his snowball and slid down the slope. But before he made the descent, he turned to me and asked my name. Then he was gone. The snow had taken him to a different place, a different world. They later found his body under the ice, but it was too late.

Uncle Joe, my mother's youngest brother, was buried in a devastating avalanche a long time ago. He was completely submerged in the icy mass and it took the dogs a long time to locate his body. Uncle Joe loved the snow, but he could not stay underneath it for so long. Uncle Joe and a few of his friends always went to Switzerland to ski. Mom said that he was a very good skier and he was a daredevil who enjoyed the deep snow. One day, he skied alone and then he met a tragic accident. Since then, Mommy never went skiing again. Father never skied and I always had to stay home to keep him company.

Snow is a mystery in itself. Even a spider's deathly web can be masked as a soft, white fluff that no insect could resist.

There were times when my Father allowed me to stay under the shed and look at the falling snow. He told me not to wander off; snow was dangerous for clumsy feet. Please snow! Let me be with you and we can both dream in silence. The flakes cover everything and it freezes my buttocks. Snow can mask grief and it can also heal and purify.

When I was very young, I caught snow in my red plastic bucket and kept it in my room. I waited for some miracle to transform it back to the enchanting white flakes that I loved so much but it never did. Nothing is permanent in life. Everything is all right until it is broken.

The approaching postman is a faint dot against the white landscape. His entire suit- sleeves, cap and jacket are all covered with snow. He gets off his bike and opens our mailbox. The snow hesitantly falls on his bike's saddle. He rubs his hands together after putting in the mail. He mounts back to his saddle and rides away.

Peter, out pet robin is the first to explore the snow-covered garden. He makes a path on the snowy land as if he is building a path for himself. He then flies all the way to the mailbox and puffs out his orange chest. Show off!

I can no longer feel my hands or my buttocks. Dad says that I have no need for gloves. He says that I can put my hands in my pockets to keep them warm. The cold weather makes you strong; he tells me that it can kill bacteria. Sometimes my father makes me walk barefoot in the snow while he holds a stopwatch in his hands. I have to endure the icy path for six minutes, but five minutes will do for a weak girl like me. I have to be tough. Father watches me from the window with his thick jacket and green turtleneck. After six long minutes, I can put my socks and boots back on. My feet are cold and my teeth chatter. My entire body shivers from the exposure but I do my best to hide it from father. If he notices, he will make me endure the cold longer.

I am so terrified that I could not even hear my own breathing. I hear father furiously tapping his signet ring on the window. I guess he had been standing there for a while and I did not notice or hear him. He is once again wearing a ridiculous turtleneck underneath a brown vest. He angrily points to the mailbox. His great mustache trembles from his rage. He wants me to retrieve the mail this instant. I do not get it immediately he will surely throw a fit.

I make the icy trek towards the mailbox. I cannot keep father waiting. He gets nervous when I take the first step. I cautiously inch my boots forward and I hear the snow crunch under my feet. I feel guilty. I'm sorry snow. We'll play later, okay?

I stand on my tiptoes to open the lid (Father put the mailbox too high) and take out two envelopes. I notice that my hands hurt from the cold even if I kept them in my pockets. I attempt to stuff the letters into my pocket but father once again pounds on the window in protest. He motions that I have to hold the envelopes in my hands. He points his index finger to his head and he makes that gesture whenever he is mad at me. I hold the mail in my hand as I run towards the door. It slips through my fingers and now the envelopes are wrinkled. Father will surely angry. He yanks the door open and snatches the mail from my hands.

3

"Come on in and out of the freezing snow."

I brush the snow off his coat and help him to his feet. His knees get strained from the stretch. "Lend me a hand," he asks. He stumbles up the stairs.

"Careful, it's slippery," I cautioned.

Fortunately he weighs lighter that before. Age has definitely worn him down.

"Hi there! Is there anything I can do to help?" my nosy next-door neighbor called out. She always looked out her window whenever I went out or came back inside my house. She constantly watched me like I was a helpless kid. I know she means well, but I don't trust her. I suspect that she has a crush on father. That old bag! She is far too small and crooked. Maybe she was abused as a child and she never had a man in her life. She might even be ridden with rheumatism. She is totally pathetic and I couldn't care less. I pretend not to hear her as we walk up the steps.

Most people cannot be trusted. I prefer to be alone with my paintings and sculptures rather than mingle with others. I am unlike Paul who is very sociable. You create art for others to appreciate. An image exists to satisfy an individual. I consider my artwork as my family. I talk to them and they give meaning to my existence.

I put down my AH shopping bag and unlock the door. I always leave the radio on when I am out to ward off burglars. The music fools them into thinking that I am at home. I wipe my feet on the "Welcome" mat on the corridor. The hallway is usually dark and yesterday it reeked of cauliflower since I ate cauliflower with lump sauce. I immensely enjoyed the meal, but I now despise the after smell. The exhaust has not been repaired and it's too cold to open a window so the odor lingered inside the house.

"Take off your coat and come to the kitchen. Do you want coffee?"
Three coats now hang on the rack. . My red and white scarf is on top of the other items. Father can have the coat rack to himself soon. I have my suitcase packed and ready at the end of the corridor. Father does not know that I am leaving.

He fumbles on the buttons of his thick winter coat. I see him impatiently squirm as he unbuttons his coat. His fingers used to play Chopin but now his fingers are hurries and nervous, as if they do not know what to do.

I gently repeat my instruction, and I do not scold him like he did when he taught me how to play the piano. I think that he was disappointed when my fingers did not find the right key. He hit the key with a stick and I got even more confused. He hit it more often and it did not help. My fingers had a mind of their own. Father was furious. He bought the piano so he could teach me how to make music. He even hit my fingers with a stick until he ran out of patience and eventually surrendered. He expected that I would share his love for music, but he had to play his painful yet beautiful compositions by himself.

I do not own a piano. Once I dreamt of owning one so I could give it to him when I was old enough and I lived on my own. However, the memory of the painful piano lessons scarred me for life. I remembered the pain as I sat on the stool while Father broke the piano in half with an axe. He was so disappointed.

He is now sixty two years old. The once smart man could no longer tie his shoelaces or put on his coat unassisted or even unbutton his shirt.

Meanwhile, I hang my padded winter coat on the rack. I try on the Nepal hat and arrange my hair as I look into the mirror. My checks are flushed from the effort. Father is still struggling with his coat. Apparently the zipper on his collar is stuck. His face is an unreadable mask that you cannot see any expression that can indicate his emotion. He does not even look angry. I unzip my fur boots and sink my feet into Eskimo slippers with real fur. I indulge on the beautiful brown softness that I was denied as a child because they were too expensive. I understood the message and did not make a fuss about it.

4

"How much is one and one?" my father asked.

I was a child, barely eight years old.

"How much is one and one?" he repeated.

"Two," I proudly answered as I handed him the envelopes.

"You're wrong, you retard. You haven't learned anything from school. Are you really that stupid? One and two, depending on the context. Hello? If I put a lump of sugar in a glass of water, are there two lumps or two parts water? No." He yanks at my ear but I do show him my pain. "It becomes a new substance. If your mother and I copulate we are one. Two become one. Look at me when I am talking to you. A left shoe and a right shoe form one pair: two become one. Use your brain, if you have any. You cannot even deliver the mail to me. I cannot wait until you move out of the house and out of my life!"

My eardrums vibrate from the pain of his punishment and the sting of his words. I hope Mom comes back in two nights just like she promised.

I try my best to utter an apology even if I am dazed. "I'm sorry, Father." He gets even more infuriated. He gives me a slap, and then he retreats into a corner like he was scalded when he beat me. He stares into space and remains tight lipped for hours. He sits motionless like a doll; you could not even hear him breathe. If he gets offended, he crawls into a chair and into himself. I think he drifts off somewhere to dream. Mom says that I am a dreamer just like him.

I try to sneak out of the living room, but he sees me escape. He grabs me hard and drags me into a chair. He commands me to put down my pants and puts me over his thighs and he beats me with a lash that he keeps under the chair. After the beating he pushes me away and if I attempt to pull up my pants he threatens me again: "I'll teach you a lesson with two loud smacks!"

I go upstairs to my room. I am safe in my room. I sat on the chair near the window and I could see the snow once again. There is a blanket of snow on the shed and at the front door. Billions of flakes make a blanket of snow. Father's right.
Beau runs through the pasture and across the neighbor's lawn. He makes crazy jumps as he hide his nose in the white, icy powder. A black dog amidst the white snow. Moments later, he runs after Knakkie, the cat with a dent on his tail. Snow scatters in all directions. Knakkie takes flight to a tree and drops lumps of snow on the Beau's muzzle. He barks even louder. I hope father is not disturbed by the ruckus. I shush him with my finger. "Quiet Beau, or Father will shoot you dead."
I stand on the chair and imagine that I am a snowflake. I whirl in the air as I look for a nice landing. Sometimes I feel so light that I have to hold onto the chair to my balance. I wish I was a snowflake; then I won't be so alone.

I hear the door open and Father storms down the trampled snow.

"Snow, rubbish. Dirty mess. I hate snow! It makes a big mushy mess when you walk back in. I wonder why some fool created it in the first place. It is meaningless."

He screams at Beau who barks even louder. Stop Beau, stop it this instant!

Father makes a snowball and throws it at the dog. Beau wags his tail and he wants to play with father. Father throws another snowball and Beau is enjoying the game. Beau runs towards him and almost hit father's chin with his paws. Father tries to shoo him away. I hear him barking louder and louder. His dirty legs have smeared Father's jacket.

Once there was dog poop in our path. I'm certain it wasn't Beau's doing, but some other dog might have wandered in our yard. Father stepped on the poop and he did not notice it until he reached the house and noticed the stench. He made me clean the floor and he threw away his stinky slippers.

Father walks back to the front door but Beau jumps on his vest.

"Go away you damn dog!"

Father falls to the ground with his back and Beau jumps on top of him. His tail wags as he begins to lick his face. Father pushes him away with his hands and one of his slippers get loose.

"Come Beau, here doggie!" I think one of the neighbors called him. Beau stops licking Father's face and runs to the farm across the street. Father scrambles to his feet, brushes the snow off his pants and frantically looks around in search for his other slipper. A few minutes later, he slams the door as he enters the house. I still love my father.

I come down a few minutes later and I see Father listening to the radio. I better keep my mouth shut so he will not be disturbed.

"Wim Sonneveld died from cardiac arrest," I hear the news on the radio. "They tried to revive him with CPR but it was too late."

"Well, another flicker less."

Father mutters to himself. He turns off the radio and grabs his puzzle book. I'm glad he's busy with his puzzles, he will ignore me.

I walk to the kitchen to make a glass of lemonade and I dare not ask him if he wants one. I carefully close the refrigerator and get some water from the tap. I softly stir the glass with a spoon. I take a sip and walk back to my room. Just as I grab the doorknob, Father tells me: Why did you not tell me that you were thirsty? Give me that glass!" I give him the glass of lemonade and he empties the glass even if he does not like it at all.

"Go back to your room."

I no longer want lemonade. I have to think of others before I think of myself.

5

I walk into the kitchen to make coffee. Father prefers tea but I go right ahead with my choice. I call Paul while I wait for the coffee to brew. He tells me that he is on his way. Father is still stuck in his coat in the hallway.

"Having trouble with your coat? Here, let me help you." I take his arm and lead him to the living room.

"Come, sit down."

I sit him on the couch next to the red gas heater. I unbutton his collar and remove the green scarf from his neck. His turkey neck annoys me. It makes him weak and wobbly. His Adam's apple is deformed from the countless folds on his neck. I think of the gruesome fate that befalls turkeys come Christmas and I decide to put the scarf back on his neck. I tie the scarf so that it would make him look stately as possible. I set his hand on the table. His hair is unruly and he stares inwards.

Paul tells me that hate does not solve anything; resentment will only eat all your organs. I should stop destroying him because he was already broken years ago. Who would have thought that I could get what I want?

I need to give forgiveness a space in my heart. I have to be strong enough to forgive my father. Paul make it look like it's easy as a breeze. As long as I nurture the hatred for my father he will always define my life and that has to stop. I know Paul is right, but I can't seem to let go…

My baby pictures line the table beside his chair. I have photos where I wear my hair in pigtails, while in others, my hair is loose. I have pictures taken in school and I even have my arms around a girl while we are in the swimming pool. I loved that picture. The only pose missing is the one where I am in my father's lap. He could not stand public displays of affection. He never received a pat on the head from his father and he grew up thinking that men must be cold and distant. Sometimes Mom called me so she could read me stories and I happily climb on her lap.

I normally keep the baby pictures in a basket under my bed, but I thought it would be nice to display them while Father is with me for two or three weeks. Who knows? Maybe he might notice them.

"You're just a stupid kid."
He always meant that statement. I heard the phrase everyday and I resented hearing it as a child. I eventually learned to live with his perception. I wore crazy clothes and I had a stupid nose. My nose was too small to hold up my glasses. What can I do? Kids in school always teased me because of my brown skin. They told me that I was born a smear and though I had red blood like theirs, I would always be inferior. I had no girlfriends. I did not have any friends. Beau was my only friend, but he was not immortal.

"Your father is your therapy." Paul said. "Once you learn to be nice to your dad you'll be healed and your life will be much better. But as long as you abhor him, he will still manipulate you. Forgiveness will set you free. Put all your resentment in a balloon and let it float away from your life. Learn to let go. Translate your sorrow into works of art-give it shape, draw a picture. You will soon see it vanish from your soul. Lies are your weakness and others will enjoy your suffering. Your purpose is to overcome angst, and that is why you are here."

Paul has told me this hundreds of times.

Today is my first day of therapy and I have to do it for an entire week. Paul will come over to daily check my progress. I have to transform resentment into understanding, much like a caterpillar morphs into beautiful butterfly. Empathy is the best remedy that can change the whole world.

I cannot find anything lovable with my father but I must not make him look evil. Paul tells me that I have to be brave and make a stance. I believe he even quoted Immanuel Kant when he told me that my behavior must be governed with a higher motive. Imagine if everyone was able to transcend their anger? That is my compass. I cannot repay the world by becoming like my father. If I am broke, the world is torn as well.

Paul arrives a few minutes later. He asks my father: "What is your name?"
Father stares at me for help. I am silent.
"May I ask how old you are?'
I could tell that he was embarrassed!
"Paul, ask him how much is one and one."

Paul frowns at the bizarre question. He is already putting on his jacket because he needs to go.

"No, really!"

"Mr. Backs, if I may ask, when is your date of birth?"

He remains silent and he glares at me. He's playing dumb as he stares on the TV. I do not remember how his voice sounds like. I only remember the sarcasm in his tone. It is etched in my head. The few sentences that he spoke to me now dance around me as ghosts. They blur my vision and mar my thoughts. I cannot think clearly, all I hear is Father's voice directing me. And I do not want to be like him.

"How about one and one, Mr. Backs. How much is one and one?" Paul tried.

His mouth is like under his Einstein-like mustache.

I decide to get up and ask him. "Father, do you want some coffee?"

Paul follows me into the kitchen.

"Are you okay?"

"I'm feeling a lot better and I'll feel better and better until I will become clean again, eh Paul?"

"Hang in there, okay?" Paul replies. "Bring him with you when you go out and when I come back, we'll decide what to do next."

Paul can only spare a moment for the visit. When he leaves, I give dad a piece of the Japanese flag.

6

Father used to take me to school because Mommy had to go to work. She was always busy with work. Mommy is a scholar. I do not know what she investigates, but she often goes abroad- Spain, Egypt, Brazil, India and China to discover things. Sometimes she's away from a month. I hardly see her at home. She has more important things to do than play with me.

Father disapproves of her trips. Mom says that the Japanese camp damaged him so much that's why he doesn't want to talk about it. She tells me to be a good kid and be obedient to him. When he gets mad, I have to say "I'm sorry, Father" and then I can go to my room.

I am happy when I am in my little room. It is my own space and my dreams are most beautiful when I am alone. I see the pasture and the stars through my window and I can float across the universe. I often visit other countries and I accompany Mom in her explorations. I encounter new scents and colors brighten my ideas. I cherish these dreams and they are mine forever.

Father is unaware that Mom has filled my locker with books. She promised to read them to me when she comes back home. I have learned to read by myself and I have read some

of the books she gave me. Father thinks that books are a waste
of time and money.

There is a booklet about China from Mom's recent trip.
It has old pictures and she reads it to me as Father takes
his afternoon nap. Mom tells me that the Chinese are very
friendly; they have a large country with a high wall around
it. "But it's crazy there, they kill learned men," Mom said.
"The clever people were buried alive and the soldiers burned
all the books about history. The only books that were allowed
were books about agriculture, medicine and astrology. Only
the emperor had access to these books." I do not understand
why she went to China.

She tells me that there are a lot of people in China; they are
as innumerable as the stars. She tells me that most of the men
in China are soldiers. She found an entire army of soldiers
buried under the soil. They were made of clay and they were
replicas of the Emperor's soldiers. Their weapons were real
and sharp, that you could get hurt if you touched the tip of the
blades. Mom says that the clay soldiers were a thousand years
old.

Father inspects my clothes. My skirt hangs below the knees
and past my white crochet socks. Father believes that bare legs
makes boys crazy and they cannot be trusted. Most people
cannot be trusted because they behave like animals. He looks
at me once again to make sure that the buttons on my dress are
properly fastened and my shoes are clean.

"Open your mouth. Did you brush your teeth? Good, we
can go."

Our house is on Ferdinand Huycknaan on the outskirts of the village. It is in front of our farm and beside the road. We go out the back door. The school is half an hour away but Father is always in a rush. His long strides make his shoes shine as he marches on the pavement. We go around the bend towards the Church on Cross Street. It is a busy street with an elevated sidewalk.

"Hurry up or else we will be late."

I try to keep up with him and I ask him if he could hold my hand but he thinks it's childish. "You're not in kindergarten anymore," he would say. Then he would get angry at me. I do not know what happened to him in the prison camp because he never gives me answers when I ask him about it.

My legs hurt as I catch up with him. I feel relieved when he meets Miss Paardekoper because he slows down his pace.

"What's the rush? We have all the time in the world," He would say. "Lizzie, are you coughing?" He would add. It's like I'm hearing someone else call my name.

"How nice of you to notice! You have a very caring dad, Lizzie. Indian people are the sweetest." Miss Paardekoper gives me a peck on the cheek and she gives my Father a pat on the shoulder. She smells like a nice perfume. Father also splashes on some cologne behind his ears and wrists from a white bottle labeled Tabac, but it smells nothing like tobacco that Father hates so much.

Father walks alongside Miss Paardekoper while I walk between him and Marit, a girl from my class. We walk together as one family.

My legs look better compared to Marit's, but Father does not notice.

"Wow, you smell good," Father tells her as he gets his nose close to her ears.

"Lovely. Do you smell everyone?" she asks.

Father laughs and so does Miss Paardekoper. I have never seen Father smile before. This is the first time that I see his teeth. His eyes narrow when he laughs and his mustache stretches. We take a leisurely stroll and I can easily keep up with them.

Miss Paardekoper lives on a big farm at the end of Ferdinand Huycklaan. Father, Mother and I visited her once. Her house has five rooms and Marit has a huge bedroom and a game room. She does not have any siblings and like me, she is an only child. She lives with her mother in that big house. Miss Paardekoper has a large studio where she creates images of wood and stone. She also makes sculptures of horses and other crazy figures from rusted iron. She told me that I could come over to her house and make my own creations.

I see pictures everywhere. I talk to them, much like I talk to the cacti in our neighbor's yard. Each cactus is a picture in itself. I see happy plants that love to float and dance. I think everything in this world had been painted but you could use the image and turn it into something different. I would love to paint Mom and Dad someday.

Father wants me to anywhere except at Miss Paardekoper's. He told me that I could visit Grandma Moes instead.

The adults let us run the last stretch near the school because they think we're good girls. But Marit and I do not run to school together. She makes a mad dash towards the school and leaves me behind because she does not want to be seen with me. She is embarrassed by my skirt, my stockings, my glasses, my ears and my brown skin. She thinks I'm stupid.

I turn around when I reach the school grounds but Father and Miss Paardekoper are gone. Marit is already with her friends while I am all alone. I am always alone, but I think being alone is better than having friends. I imagine Beau is with me and I watch him do tricks and when the bell rings, I send him home.

Miss Paardekoper and Marit often come to our house. "You two go and play in Lizzie's room," Father sends us away with his unusually sweet voice. But I would rather stay with Miss Paardekoper than play.

Once we are in my room, Marit tells me: "You do not have a real father. My mom tells me that you are adopted."

She grabs my doll and when I resist, she screams at me and pulls at my hair. She gets the scissors from her pocket and cuts off my doll's hair on one side. She laughs as she lowers her scissors and rips my doll's stomach open. Then she throws my mutilated doll in a corner.

"What an ugly doll. Nobody will play with it now."

I know I can fix my doll and put her back together with some tape.

When they leave, Marit gets to take home a pink bath.

"Here, Marit. You can use this to give your doll a bath."

I start to cry.

"They need to learn not to get too attached to things. Attachment is not good."

"I think Lizzie's doll is nice." Marit adds as she slid her arm around my father's.

"Sure, you can keep it." Father says. "Lizzie, go and get your doll."

I stomp up the stairs in anger and I hold her up to show that she's broken.

"Please don't take my doll!"

"I do not want her doll. It looks silly," Marit exclaims.

"I'll buy you a doll," Miss Paardekoper tells her.

Father locks me inside the closet once the visitors walk out the door. "I saw you crying because of your things. Those are not important!"

It is dark inside the closet, but I make out some shapes as my eyes adjust to the dark. I feel a broom, a mop and a bucket. I pull out my China book and read it with a flashlight. He can scream at me for as long as he wants but I do not hear him while I am in faraway China.

I pretend that the closet is filled with an entire Chinese clay army. I stand straight and hold the broom as my weapon. I imagine that I am a Chinese warrior. I touch the tip of the broom. It is very sharp just like the tip of a soldier's sword. I look around and see tens of thousands of soldiers. We are many and we are a powerful army! Our empire continues to grow and soon, we will rule the world!

I thrust my sword when suddenly the closet door opens. The broom's tip hits my father in the belly. I did not hear him coming and did not hear him turn the lock. He grabs me from the closet and drags me into the living room.

"You silly child! I'll teach you to behave!"

He jabs the broom into my belly but I do not even wince at the pain. He pushes it further but I do not cry. A warrior does not shed tears.

"I'm sorry, Dad. It was an accident. I didn't know you were at the door."

My sincere apology infuriates him. He whips my butt with a stick until he is too exhausted to continue. But I still do not cry. I wait until I am in my room and there I break into sobs.

Master Wilkenman's class is no fun. He speaks very fast and he spews out saliva. His dictated words do not make any sense. I need to read the book so I can understand. Sometimes he twists my ear and asks me: "Are you deaf?" He is just like father. I'm the only one in class who has trouble hearing. Marit tells me I'm deaf. Ada makes it worse. She tells the class that I am both deaf and dumb. They all laugh at me. But I do well in Math and Reading. My grades are quite good, but Father insists that I can do better. I want to be a scholar when I grow up, but I am afraid that I might be buried alive.

7

My Dad and I watch some television. I have to put him to bed after the news; otherwise he will doze off in his chair. But there's a football game tonight and I am an Ajax fan. Father loves football too although he was ashamed to admit it at first. But when he discovered that it was a national sport and Baron van Hees was playing for Panneyden, he confessed he was crazy about the sport.

I know what I have to do. I need to forgive him and let go of all the hurt. That's what Paul has advised me.

The Olympic Stadium is jam packed and many people are tuned into the game. I give dad a piece of cake with pink frosting. I put it on a saucer and set it on the table with a fork close to where I displayed my baby pictures. I pour myself a cup of coffee. I decide not to tease Father and I give him a glass of water to drink with his cake.

We first watch the news. Father tells me that fifty years ago, the Americans dropped bombs on the Japanese cities of Hiroshima and Nagasaki. He has become restless with war all these years. I break off a piece of cake with the fork and put it before his mouth. He must remain calm otherwise we will miss the game.

Nelson Mandela was freed by Dekerk and he won the Nobel Peace Prize but my father remains cold and distant.

I go for a bathroom break after the news is over. When I return to the living room, I find him slumped on the chair full of crumbs. I brush the pieces of cake from his trousers and sit him upright.
"Try to relax and enjoy the game." I wet my palms with spit and comb the stray strands into place.
"You can sit here in the dais in front of the tube!" He did not respond. He used to drum a pencil with his fingers to keep him busy. He also sat cross legged on the chair as he stared into the distance. When his legs wobbled, he knew that it was time to shift his legs. Unfortunately, he does not have a pencil and all he can do is rest his hands on the arm chair.

The game has barely begun and we are already behind, 0-1. Father is not worried. He remains confident that we will win the game. After a quarter, Ajax is down by a huge margin, 0-4. He is silent. I turn off the TV. In my mind, I hear him say that Germans are no good; they are like the Japs. He used to play football. I push the table a little further and clean up the mess because he spilled his tea.

I take his hand and lead him to the guest room. He is content with the air mattress for his bed. I put his coat back on and drape a quilt over him because it's cold inside the room. I do not have central heating and the ground is frozen. I normally dry my clothes in the room but I had to accommodate Father so I temporarily removed the laundry rack so he would not see my undies.
I see beautiful ice crystals on the window and they remind me of the fossils that Mom found.

"Sleep well, I'll see you tomorrow!"

I close the curtains and turn off the light. I close the door behind me and I get ready for bed. In contrast, Father never tucked me in. I look into the bathroom mirror while I turn on the light and the shower. Paul changed the light bulb and the newly installed light reveals the wrinkles on my face even when I am only 27. I've never been happier in my life. I cannot imagine that I made a fuss over my looks when I was the prettiest girl during our senior year. People often told me that I was insecure over nothing.

I take a long hot bath and lathe pink shower gel in a sponge. Tomorrow is a new day. I have to be nice to him again because he has suffered so much.

I put on my pajamas and think about my Mom who is currently in India. I wonder how she is doing. I read a fascinating book about Jan Gooseren. He makes paintings differently and I am very interested in his work. Maybe I can get inspiration from his work and someday we can work together. His intriguing mix of straight lines and round shapes engages me. A tight horizon with a round sun, straight redwoods with the silver moon in the background. Soft and hard. Contrasts have always appealed to me. Jan is a gifted artist. He is a connoisseur in his own right. The man is simply brilliant!

I remove my hearing aid but opt to keep the socks so my feet would stay warm through the night.

"Good night, Lizzie." I say to myself as I pull the covers over my head.

8

I get to spend an entire day with Miss Paardekoper even if Father does not approve. Marit is not around and she has time to teach me art lessons.

"We will start with clay," Miss Paardekoper tells me. "Clay is flexible."

She is wearing a long blue apron that covers her bare legs. She has cute yellow sneakers on her feet while I am dressed in old clothes in case I get dirty. I wear Capri pants and there are holes on the elbows of my sweater. My sweater smells like Mom. I brought some clean clothes in a bag so I could change after the lesson.

"Try to feel the clay," she instructed. "What do you feel?"

I do not know what to say but the clay feels greasy and cold.

"It feels greasy cold." I shyly answer. I do not want her to laugh at my response.

"You've made a beautiful description of the clay-greasy cold."

She picks a different stuff.

"Now, feel this. Sculpting and modeling begins with feeling."

I grab a chunk of the gray matter. It feels cold, but not greasy. How will I describe it?

"I feel coarse grains. It feels bumpy," I said.

"That's grog," Miss Paardekoper tells me. "It is specially designed for modeling and frying. How about this?"

She gives me a square gunk. I squeeze it well.

"I can feel lumps, but finer. It feels graceful."

"Good, you describe it with special words. You are very sensitive and you feel very well. This is fire fine clay while the other is coarse clay. Do you know that not everyone can feel as good as you do? To make beautiful artwork, you need to lover your material. You must own it as you mold it with your fingers. Your eyes and your hands must work together as one. You'll soon learn to sculpt with feeling. You will become an expert when your hands move faster than your brain. You will use your head later to assess your work. Which material do you want for your first project?"

I chose the refined clay.

"The second thing that you must learn is observation. Once you have discovered how to see and feel, you start making real art. Many people do not develop this talent. They hesitate to touch strange things and they choose to see what they only want to see."

She picks up a picture book and points to a drawing of a box.

"Lizzie, do you have any idea what this is?"

I do not dare to say anything. I am certain that it is a die without dots.

"Well?"

"I see a box, a cube." I now feel ashamed.

"No," she puts her arm around me. "You do not see a box. Can you put something in it?'

I shake my head. I find her question a bit odd. It's just a page of a book.

"Look harder. Do you really see a cube or do you see lines that look like a cube?"

She turns the page and asks me if I see straight or curved lines. I see curves. She hands me a ruler and asks me to check if the lines are indeed straight or wavy. The lines are remarkably straight and the lines are surprisingly of the same length.

"Do you understand how difficult it is to see? Do you notice how the area of these lines and the context distorts reality? If I make oblique lines around a circle the lines appear curved. If I draw look at the diagonal lines at the end, the lines appear somewhat shorter like a roof. If I draw the line gently upward, I see a letter "V" and the line seems longer. As artists, we have a different perception of reality. Perhaps we are the only ones who see reality while other people are blind to it.

I do not understand what she is saying.

"Lizzie, is there something that you enjoy watching?" She asked.

No one has ever asked me so many questions but I do not find them obstrusive. She puts her arm around me once again. Her arms feel velvety soft. She presses my head on her belly.

"Come on; let's sit down for a while."

There is an old red sofa with yellow pillows and a purple chair in the studio. Paintings hang from the walls and sculptures are everywhere. The room has a high ceiling with a beam in the center. A bird cage hangs in the center of the beam. I think that a parrot once lived in the cage. It is adorned with a colorful necktie! The back wall is entirely made of glass. The huge windows give a panoramic view of the pasture.

We sit together on the couch. She smells good. Her black ponytail waves in a funny way when she nods her head back and forth as she speaks. She looks at me with kind eyes. I think she and Mom are of the same age.

"Do you like to watch anything?"

What should I say? I spent most of my time staring out of the window, looking at the pasture, Beau and the birds as they move across the grass and snow. I gaze up to the stars. She detects that I am hesitant and I am afraid that she might see me as a stupid child of ten who stammers when she speaks.

"Do you want to know what I love watching? People- old and young alike. I think that people are most beautiful when they are naked and exposed. They cannot hide behind a dress or a suit. I had tough soldiers who were confident and even arrogant in their uniforms but they all withered in my studio especially when they were stripped of their underpants. They were mere boys when disarmed. You know what? Girls and women are more willing to let go of their clothes than men."

She puts her hand on my knees and asks again: "And you, Lizzie, what do you like?"

I look around and see the people that she described. I see naked and bare men, shy and exposed old men (is that Father I see?). I also see beautiful, naked men. I have never seen anyone else naked except myself. I see a nude painting of Miss Paardekoper. She appears to be standing in front of a mirror. She has slender legs, a round belly and full, round breasts. Who painted her?

"I like snow. I love snow."

I lower my eyes with my confession. I hope that she will not laugh at me. I feel like I am naked as well. She stands up and walks over to the plastic shelf were she keeps her clay.

"You're a very special girl, Lizzie."

She grabs a lump of clay and kneads it with her hands.

"I have given lessons to people of all ages, from seven to thirty and not one has ever mentioned snow. You are a remarkable character- unusual, fresh and original in a naïve way. I will ask your father to let you come over every weekend. Do you like that? I think that you are an artist. Art is inside you and you can make the world a more beautiful place with your creativity. Come on, Lizzie, we're going to make something beautiful together."

We each get a lump of clay.

"Knead it first then you can shape it afterwards." We mold the clay into various forms.

I like clay. It does what I want, it listens to me.

I try to make a boy rolling a snowball. His knees are slightly bent as he holds on to the ball. I am unaware that my fingers are moving on their own. I make the figure for more than an hour. I feel like I am back in the snow with my old friend. I immortalize my long-gone boyfriend in clay.

Miss Paardekoper loves it.

"He lives!" she exclaims. "I will bake it for you then you can come over and take him home next week. Are you hungry? Do you want to eat anything?"

What do I want? No one has asked me before what I want. Why does she need to ask me what I want to eat?

She kisses me on the cheek and puts her hand on my shoulder. She feels softer than before.

"Pancakes? Do you want to make pancakes? With ham, cheese, apple, raisins, banana or whatever you want to put in it."

She steers me into the kitchen where there is a huge table good enough for six people. Her arm is still on my shoulder. I want to push it aside, but I do not dare. She sees my anxiety.

"Do not be afraid, I won't eat you! Wait, my lipstick left a smudge on your cheek."

She wipes off the stain from my face. I find it scary when she touches me but it feels nice to be touched. I guess I'm not used to it.

We make the batter together. I put in some eggs and sugar and flour and I pretend to be a magician. She has the most fun. "Huppekee...plop...plop...tata!" She makes playful sounds that make me laugh. When it is time to turn the pancakes, she flips it high in the air and gracefully catches it with the pan. I try to imitate her, but three of my pancakes land on the floor. We both think it's hilarious. I try a few more time and pretty soon we have a he stack of pancakes in front of us.

We sit on the table to enjoy our snack. She rolls her pancake with her fork after she drizzles it with syrup. I try to do the same to my pancake.

"Just puncture the ends and then roll it with a fork like this."

After a few tries, I succeed with rolling my pancake. Then she cuts her pancake in half and I do follow her lead.

"How's your father, Lizzie? Is he feeling better?" Miss Paardekoper asks.

I shrug my shoulders. "I don't know. He never tells me anything. I immediately regret saying those words. I do not mean to say bad things about Father. Miss Paardekoper thinks that he is a nice man. I saw how he smiled when she playfully hit him on the shoulder.

She stares at me for a long time. Great, I screwed everything.

"Did you ever sit on your father's lap?"

I gently shake my head. I cannot recall sitting on his lap. I only remember sitting on Mom's lap when she reads me stories. Then I could smell Mom's perfume and feel her soft hands. I like sitting on her lap but she is always away. I do not think Dad ever touched me in a nice way. He only touched me when he hit me or whipped me with a stick.

"Marit tells me that I'm adopted. She tells me that he is not my real Father."

I am instantly sorry that I told on Marit.

"But Marit doesn't have a father, either. Right? I mean, you live alone in this house."

What's happening to me? I sit on the table and I am supposed to eat pancakes but then I say the craziest things. She'll definitely throw me out of the house.

I let Marit take my toys, but I could not bear to see her take away my father as well.

Miss Paardekoper invites me to the meadow after dinner.

"We're going barefoot," she says. "So you can feel the grass. Feeling is important, remember?"

Of course I remember! We walk for a while and then she lies down on the grass as she faces the sky. She has red nails on her feet.

"Lizzie, come lie down next to me. Then we will feel and see."

I think it's a crazy idea but I keep my mouth shut.

"Come a little closer," she urged.

She points up to the sky.

"What do you see?"

I see white clouds with an orange border that it seems that a tiny lamp was ignited in heaven. A small cloud drifts away. I am that cloud, and I am floating towards Mom. The rest of the sky is a clear blue.

"We are now on the green grass under the blue sky. Do you think that green and blue go together?" She continued to look at the sky and she did not even bother to look at me when she asked me the question. Of course they fit together. It's been there for ages. She spoke again before I could answer her.

"Green and blue and red are primary colors. They are the main colors so to speak. In the past, it was absurd to pair a green blouse with a blue skirt but come to think of it, these colors have co-existed together for centuries. Orange and red may not be used together because they were loud colors. It's as if nature swears with these two colors. Remember Lizzie, people can do all the talking and when artists combine colors the experts find it disgusting. Experts, ha! They try to dictate how colors should be used. But after some time, they get used to the colors and realize that the work is brilliant. An artist will not make something that will please other people, unless you want to make a lot of money."

She looks at me and gives me a sweet smile.

"You have to make whatever you want to make, even if everyone else thinks it's ugly. You know what, Lizzie? If you only make what pleases other people, then you will never learn how to live. You do not need to be like everyone. You have to be yourself!"

I feel comforted with her words. I have tried to blend in and adapt so I would be unnoticed. But I can be me! But I do not know who I really am.

Miss Paardekoper can be a little crazy, but she is a lot of fun.

We run our hands along the tips of the grass. Then she plucks a blade and caresses it. It feels smooth and rough at the same time. It is flexible and sharp. Grass can turn into milk and cats can choke on a blade of grass. I knew that there are many types of grass.

"Try to look at everything else like you do with snow. Looking is not the same as seeing," she explains. "Everyone can look but seeing belongs to artists. They are innovators. I know blind people who see far better than others. Lizzie, you are a unique visionary in a literal sense. You might think I am crazy. Most people think artists are crazy, but being normal is a burden."

I could just kiss Miss Paardekoper.

"Now let's feel our stomachs." She pulls up her blouse and feels her tummy. I follow her lead.

"Move your hand gently over your tummy. Yeah, that's it. Now give it a little pinch like you do with clay. Can you feel it?"

I dare not touch her. But she grabs my hand and rubs it on her navel. When she lets go of my hand, I give it a slight squeeze.

"Do you feel the difference of tummy of ten and a belly of almost forty? Mine is rounded and fatter, isn't it? Your legs are harder than mine."

She moves my hand to her thigh.

"Do you feel how soft it is? Men's thighs are a lot harder. That's because of the adipose tissue and the muscles in their legs."

She stands up abruptly.

"Come on," she calls. "We will go back to the studio and we will see if you can spot the difference in the paintings. Lizzie, do you know that it is difficult to express emotions in a painting?

9

The weather is nice and fresh even if the sun is not shining. I sit Father on the stairs of my apartment. There is a bottle of water beside him in case he gets thirsty. He cannot go jogging, so he needs to be content with sitting on the stairs even if he cannot stay out too long in 'the sun.'

I occasionally take a peek from the window to make sure that he's all right. I observer the passersby as they walk past by him. Some of them look back and wonder why an old man would be sitting on the steps alone. I am amused at what I see. Each person has a unique reaction and it's as diverse as they features and their gaits. I make quick sketches of the puzzled faces and their strides. I want to capture the contrast of expressions in a sculpture. I want it to be perfect; when you look at the sculpture from a distance you will think that you're seeing an old man but when you take a closer look, you realize that it's a fresh face of a young woman. The tension in the shapes satisfies me. The figures are not what they seem as they effortlessly mesh with one another.

I make images that surprise people. I want to touch people with my art. Once I sculpted a man in the middle of the center of The Hague. He wore a long raincoat and he held a briefcase in his hands. He also wore a hat. A closer look reveals that his mind is in his forehead. Sometimes I watch how people react to the sculpture. They sit on a bench and stare at it, some walk a few times around it to grasp the idea. They do not understand what they see and they often laugh at the portrait. I also have a sculpture of a boy rolling a snowball set in the city of Groningen. He looks back at the observer as he rolls the snowball in his hands. He stares back at you with four faces at once but only one is visible. He's the guy who always looks at me. I will never forget him: my first boyfriend.

Father stares straight ahead, he is engulfed in his own fantasy. I borrowed a wheelchair so I could take him outdoors. I raise the cart with difficulty. He is utterly helpless as his hat falls off his head. I fastened a diaper on him to keep his incontinence at bay. I loosened the belt on his dark brown pants so he could be more comfortable. I put the fedora on his legs and I make sure that he is completely strapped in so he would not fall as we walk down the sidewalk. His gray hair is neatly combed and he looks very aristocratic. If it gets too cold, he can always put on his hat.

We walk along the riverbank. His tight jacket and green scarf makes him look frivolous. People think that we make an interesting pair. I have my sunglasses on and they cannot look into my eyes but I can see their expressions. I study their eyes and lips because they are the most revealing features of a person's face. A mouth that moves a millimeter downward can entirely change a person's character. A smile can be haughty and engaging at the same time. It can be a sweet smile or a hard grin. I have taken hundreds of photographs of mouths and eyes and infer a person's personality from the tell tale features.

Paul and I once visited a mental institution and I found out that the patients to be very intriguing. I took pictures of depressed and disturbed people that some even seemed dangerous. I imagined what it was like to live amongst them as I relied on their mouth and eyes to know what they were thinking but that proved to be very difficult.

I have made numerous sketches of Father. His expressionless inward gaze is very appealing. The bright green scarf does not suit him, but the unexpected contrast makes him an exciting subject. I would love to set him in a black Spanish beret with a red lining and that would him more entertaining.

I myself am in all black. Black is not a color; it is all the colors combined. My souls is extremely colorful and everything is lines with red, except for my coat which has a yellow lining.

There are a few people on the ice. The snow is not completely gone, but volunteers have cleared the snow with brooms made from a rectangular piece of wood with nails on it.

I decide to go skating with Father. Heck, why not? I slide the wheelchair across the ice and I glide alongside him. No one is watching us. I feel a bit boisterous. This is the first time that Father and I are on the ice. He never liked snow or ice.

A skater wearing a leotard and a red Santa hat with tinkling bells skates past us with long strides. He gives us a friendly nod. "Nice weather, eh?" I detect a flat Hague accent in his voice. Moments later, he turns around and skates back in our direction. "Dude, what a great idea! A wheelchair on the ice! Of course, someone who is disabled cannot be limited!" He gives me a wink and Father receives a pat on his shoulder.

"Just kidding."

The way he pronounced the word "disabled" makes Father less handicapped.

The man skates a few hundred yards away then falls hard on the ice. I think the ice cracked when he fell. He checks his knee and scrambles to get up. He skates again but with difficulty. I look at him and see that he is in pain. He touches his knee again and then looks around. But no one noticed his little accident. He glides on the ice and collides with the overhead bridge. He is sprawled on the ice. The people skate toward him and the couple on the bridge lean forward and look down at him. I too want to help, but I have my hands full with Father on the wheelchair.

I review the scene in my mind: the man fells his knee, looks back and collides with the bridge. I'm going to alter the scene and make it into a painting where the man bows low enough to make it past the bridge so he will no longer collide with it. It will be a beautiful masterpiece.

I try to get the trolley across the ice to where the boats are. There are benches along the waterfront. We pass by a houseboat and see someone watching ice skating on the television. Oddly enough, he is wearing a T-short when all the others have thick clothes. I look for a jetty and push the wheelchair in that direction. A few minutes later, I pull the wheelchair off the ice. His seatbelt keeps him intact as I struggle to push it onto the sidewalk. I suddenly slip. The cart bounces back on the ice and thankfully Father remains upright in his mobile seat. His head wobbles a little. I wish I made a collar under his scarf to keep him warmer.

An older couple conveniently skates to him while I wipe my coat and trudge back to the ice. "You are lucky," they tell me. It strikes me that people rarely notice an invalid. Once you are in a cart, you fade into the background, unnoticed.

"Be careful. The ice on the other side of the jetty is too thin. I wouldn't go there if I were you. Well, have a nice day."

I walk back to the sidewalk and spot a bench five feet away. I think that I could help Father stand up and he can do some exercise by walking. I pull the wheelchair close to me and I discover that the wheelchair is empty. Startled, I look back and see Father lying down on the cold, frozen river. His butt is on the ice while his back is on the edge of the sidewalk. I run back to the scene with the trolley. Could he have loosened his seatbelt?

No one noticed the slip. You can drop dead and no one will notice. He could have died with such a nasty fall. Good riddance, in that case. Hey, what was I thinking? His life is intertwined with mine. Death is nothing more but death. Maybe he will be reincarnated as a cruel stepfather to some poor boy.

I laugh as a guy my age or slightly older asks me if I have a light. I do not have a lighter and I do not smoke.

"Good," the guy said. "Neither do I."

"Then why did you ask me if I had a light?"

"Ah, so I would know if a beautiful woman such as you smokes or not... Can I sit with you?"

His name is Farhad, which means "happiness." He told me that he has seen me around. We live in the same neighborhood and he's into real estate. I tell him where I live and tell him that I have an art studio. He has kind eyes and it looks like he has a strong body. For the first time in my life, I feel butterflies in my stomach.

"How sweet of you to hang out with your father," he says. He briefly touches my hand. My entire body tingles from his touch.

Farhad was born in India but he migrated to The Netherlands when he was twenty. We both share the same brown complexion and dark eyes. His nose is slightly larger than mine but I think it's attractive. He is interested in homes, office buildings and cars. I give him my phone number and the address of my studio.

"I know that place," he tells me. "You make beautiful paintings."

He kisses my hand and walks away with an athletic swagger.

Then I realized that I forgot to ask him his number.

I turn to Father and urge him: "Come on, let's get some tea. You've earned it."

When we get back home, I linger in front of the mirror and study myself. I survey from face from every angle then turn around to inspect my hair and my back. My breasts and buttocks are barely visible in my jacket. I notice that the mole on my upper lip has considerably grown. I put my coat back on and look at myself for a long time. I apply a fresh coat of color on my lips though I have never worn lipstick at home.

10

I can now take my freshly bakes sculpture home. Miss Paardekoper puts it in a plastic bag from the DA drugstore. He looks playful. We called my first creation *Boy with Snowball*. Miss Paardekoper tells me that each work of art must have a name.

"You surely know the expression so it must have a name!" She burst out laughing.

"Do you know what the birdcage with the necktie is called? *Flown without noose!*"

She laughs again and I couldn't help but laugh with her.

"My ex-boyfriend is gone and so is his daughter, Marit. I immediately made it after they left. The bird has freely flown away but the rope remains: he has made her burden lighter. The piece is a reminder for me not to fall for the wrong guy again. They first shower with love and attention but they fade in the long run... why am I telling a young child about my heartaches? I'm sorry, Lizzie. I'm just a little crazy."

When I get home, I put the *Boy with Snowball* face front on the windowsill so he could see the pasture from my bedroom window. I had not seen Marit in school these past days. Miss Paardekoper did not tell me anything and I did not bother to ask her. I grab my sketchbook and draw a picture of a bird with a tie. *Marit, flown noose.* I put the title underneath. It must have a name.

School is better now that Master Winkelman is on leave. He is overworked and he has no plans of finishing the school year. We have a new teacher, Miss Vlasblom and she's really nice. She has not pinched my ear. She is a young teacher fresh out of school and she wears jeans and high heels to school. Ada is still in the classroom but she is not as mean now that Marit is gone. She prefers to ignore me. I am happy that I will soon transfer to a new school.

I think I have a new friend. She came from the Asylum Center and she is new in school. She comes from Saigon and she does not speak Dutch. The teacher told me that she would sit beside me so I could help with her schoolwork. Her name is Tuyet which mean "white as snow", although she is dark. She has black hair and tiny eyes like the Chinese. The teacher locates Vietnam on the map and brings a book with pictures that tell us about Tuyet's birthplace.

"There was a war," Miss Vlasblom tells the entire class.

"Tuyet was in a small boat with a lot of people and they sailed across the water even if it was dangerous. They hoped that a large boat would rescue them and take them to a different country so they could be safe. Luckily, a boat from The Netherlands picked them up. Now Tuyet lives with an adoptive aunt. Her siblings were in another boat and it was attacked by pirates. I'm afraid that they will not survive. Tuyet is the only one in her family who reached The Netherlands."

I feel sorry for Tuyet. I take her to her adoptive aunt after school. Her aunt works in a restaurant. We first stop by our house so I could show her my room. We slowly ease ourselves through the back door. Dad is taking his nap and he is asleep on the couch. He wakes when he hears us come in. Dad is furious when he sees Tuyet and sends her out of the house.

"Go away, you dirty gook!" He snorts. Spittle flies from his mouth. Father's entire frame violently shakes as he speaks and his face is as pale as sheet. He puts his hand to his chest. Tuyet looks at me and then run away.

Now I've lost a friend. But I still have Miss Paardekoper.

"Beat it," Dad tells her.

I ran after Tuyet. She hasn't gone far and I catch up with her. She is silent as I walk alongside her. I do not know how to explain my Father's outburst.

"I want to say sorry for what my father did a while back. He is sick and a little crazy."

I try to put an arm around her shoulder but she pushes me away. She continues to walk on the sidewalk.

"Father was once a prisoner of war in a Japanese camp." I offer so she could understand.

Tuyet shrugs. "Both my parents are dead. They were thrown overboard by pirates."

She's right. Father is not really crazy. People have their own tragic tales to tell.

"Today we are going to work with chicken wire. That will be the foundation of our image."

Miss Paardekoper points at three different images at various stages of completion. There is a figure made from wire while the other already has clay attached to the mesh. She explains: "I am always working on a few images at the same time."

"I welded a dog for you." She points to an iron statue on the table. "We call this a frame, and it works just like the way our bones and ribs do. We will fill the image with clay just like we have meat in our bones."

She cuts off part of the mesh and forms it into a dog's tail. She squeezes it in and attaches it to the frame. "See? Just follow what I said and you'll be able to complete the skeleton." We soon complete the animal's frame and though the chicken wire feels rough, it will soon go unnoticed.

"And now we will cover the frame. Unfortunately, this is the part where we get dirty."

There is a box on the table with newspapers and wall paper paste inside. We tear the newspapers into small pieces and mix it with the glue.

She dons her apron over her denim skirt. She also puts her hair up in a tight ponytail. Her eyes are darkened with mascara and her lips are bright red. The rest of her face is creamy white. I notice that she has a full mouth. Her legs are neither pale nor brown. Today she is wearing thick round glasses with a black frame. Her glasses are almost the same size as mine, but hers looks way funnier. She smells good as usual.

"Wait…" She pauses and she walks to the kitchen. "I have a coat for you."

She hands me a green coat. I am thrilled!

"I gave it so your father won't complain about the mess. Are you okay with him?"

I tell her the incident about Tuyet.

"He said that?" She could not believe her ears.

"That man is totally screwed. He has been through a lot. Did he ever tell you about his experiences as a prisoner?"

I grab a dollop of paper glue and smear it on my dog's tail.

"Constant beatings and a lot of humiliation. They often bow deeply to the Japanese; every day, every hour. They spend the entire day in sun as punishment. The children are dragged through the mud. The only thing they eat is porridge and it look like this stuff." I point to the sticky mixture.

Ben Bouter

"Come on, let's sculpt. There is enough misery in the world. We can make it brighter with a little art."

She kneads the substance longer than usual and rubs it on the dog's belly.

"You can do the rest..." She walks away without a word.

I should not have told her about Tuyet. I am such a blabbermouth.

I carefully fill the dog's tummy with paper glue. The canine's stomach has more fat than my Father's abdomen. I soon fill in the feet. It's a puppy with thick stubby legs, long, floppy ears and a wagging tail. Dogs enjoy it when humans stroke them.

According to Miss Paardekoper, the technique is called paper mache.

"Lizzie, do you have any idea what paper mache means? Do they teach you French in school?"

I pause and think. Mache...?

"Paper mache means chewed paper. People used to chew the paper to make it into paste. Then they use the paste to make dolls and stuff. Smart, eh?"

Miss Paardekoper and I drink lemonade while we sit on the red sofa. She points to a portrait of a naked man on the wall. "That's your father over there." She fondly gazes at the painting. I see an old, light brown body with a youthful face. I did not know that he had chest hair. His shiny black hair is brushed back and his eyes are smiling. He has a thin mustache. He is sitting cross legged on the purple chair.

I laugh. She's joking. That painting does not resemble my Dad.

"You don't believe me?"

She takes a picture from a drawer.

"This is what your Father looked like when he was young."
I realize that both the images have the same youthful head.
"I first painted his head based on his old photographs and he
later on posed nude in this studio. His head was full of dreams,
filled with mathematical formulas... he wanted to understand
life down to the minute of details. But the war damaged his
mind and scarred his heart. Don't you understand, Lizzie?
Fear has crippled him. He is constantly tormented by fear. He
really, really loves you but he is afraid that you will reject
him if he shows his affection. That is the reason why he is so
distant."

Miss Paardekoper grabs my hand and stands up. We walk
together to the corner of the studio where a statue stands on
a small pillar. The statue is slightly smaller than me. It is a
figure of a male with thin, long legs and a big, fat belly. This is
how a boy from the Japanese POW camp looks like. He tries
to hide his face with his bony fingers but they cannot conceal
his eyes. Your father cannot let go of his tragic past. He sees
the boy every day and it haunts him in his sleep."

She puts an arm around me and we walk back to the sofa.
Once we are seated, she points to a naked old woman. The
painting is completely white, almost translucent. Her breasts
sag like limp plastic bags. She wears white baggy underpants.
One of her arms is angled while her hair clings on her head.
She has a sweet and hopeful smile on her face.

"How about this, Lizzie. What do you think of this woman?"
I think she's beautiful. I want to say that she is beautiful.
"I wish she was my grandmother." I reply.

Miss Paardekoper cries. She holds me close to her bosom
and she strokes my head as she cries. I hear her heart crying.
She presses my head against her cheek and gives me a kiss. I
also shed tears, but I do not know why.

"I was nourished with those breasts. Those hands cared for me. My mother was once the most beautiful woman in all The Netherlands. She was a brilliant actress and I breathlessly listened to her even if she read a page from the phonebook. She continued to be a star until she was eighty.

I ask: "Is she dead?"

She takes a sip of the red stuff that does not smell like lemonade. The bottle indicates that it is Martini.

"Thank heavens, no. She is very much alive. Look at her face! She is immortal. Artists can conquer death. Our artworks whether it is made from bronze or from paint, lives longer that we do. We survive everything because we create lasting images. You see statues dating back hundreds of years before Christ in museums. Painting hang on walls for centuries while their artists have all turned to dust. Their art lives. Create something and endow it with eternal life, and you will live longer than an ordinary man."

She stares out for a moment to ponder on her mother, herself and her future.

She puts her glass down.

"And now we go back to work! Your dog is ready for a second layer of paper mache and then we're going to paint it."

11

We take a walk along the canal. A houseboat and a number of sailing ships bob on the water. I see two pleasure boats that resemble an old man's bike with a plastic bag around the saddle. The bar embraces a child's colored bicycle. My imagination runs wild. Do they have to make everything in pairs? Father and daughter? I take a closer look and see that the rack I clamped to the boat like a child clings to his father. They sway together and never let go of each other.

It reminds me of my Father.

The old city is a pleasant sight. Beautiful terraces and facades complement each other. The streets are clean and blind people will have no trouble walking. The people are no different from those in The Hague or Soestdijk, but their language is coarser. Their language is filthy like it came from a garbage truck. I do not think that this is the right place for Dad. I taste the Rotterdam Beurstraverse instead of "Boulevard." They call a suit a garb. Hands are claws, breasts are automatically tits.

"Don't judge the place too quickly," Paul tells me. "This place is very famous."

I've read about the place so I can tell Father where we are going. There are people from all over the world, including Malaysians. I honestly think that Schiedam is a nice place.

Ben Bouter

I see an alluring, stately home. The exterior is reminiscent of a blend of Nouveau and Berlage. I'm quite disappointed that the style is not what I love, but it doesn't matter. Modern art is much more colorful. The elderly are oftentimes burdened with their gloom. They grovel until death claims their souls. Sometimes I even imagine a tombstone saying: "Welcome to the land of the dying! Please do not linger, that will cost us a lot of money." I wish I could recreate spring in these drab buildings. Older people cannot get enough of the past and they no longer need a fresh outlook on things.

If Father sees a painting of Miss Paardekoper, he will surely want to live in this place.

The hall is spacious and stylish. It was lighter and fresher than I expected. There's actually art on the wall: large, modern paintings! I also see respectable ladies and gentlemen older than Father, and young nurses. Yes, he will be happy in this place.

"The nursing home is locked," Paul informed me.

The door is securely locked from the inside and you can only get in if you know the code. A friendly lady of about fifty smiles at us as she opens the door. She is wearing a light green suit like that of Queen Elizabeth's, only it is stained.

Paul tells me" "Be careful, they are so demented that they would not even know that she is letting us in."

I reply: "That sounds harsh. Maybe she is a member of the Board of Trustees."

"I'm on my way to an urgent appointment," the lady said. "I'm running late and I do not know where I left my handbag."

I realized that the stain on her suit was either from milk or yogurt.

The green suit is ruined.

62

We take a tour around the house. We peek into the living room and the bedrooms. The bedrooms can be shared by two or three people and there is nothing special inside. There are generic hospital cabinets beside the beds. They are pictures of dearly missed relatives pinned on the cabinets. I suppose these are relatives that the patients need to remember. If I had the same fate, I would gladly swallow it like a pill with a glass of Burgundy. Death is far more reason to celebrate than the slow decline. There are numerous bodies with empty minds wandering aimlessly in the hall.

Most of the people in the living room have dozed off. A man with a crooked tie is watching TV on a blank screen. His fly is open but nobody cares.

I would rather celebrate the imminent with a festival filled with dance and silly plays. I would even make a comedy and call it CliniClowns to make all these people laugh.

"Hello ma'am, sir."

A man about seventy years old, neat and with an academic voice walks towards us. He shakes our hands.

"I've been expecting you and we can discuss the terms as we go along."

He ushers us into a stately couch. He sits upright, his creased pants are impeccable while his hair is neatly combed back.

"Take a look around, I have refurbished the place- the sofa, the antique chairs, the tableware."

He is proud of his accomplishment. When he smiles, I see well-maintained teeth with a few crowns. His hair is expertly cut and even his neck hair trimmed. His ear hair is also shaved like his eyebrows. He proudly wears an Epicurean bow tie.

"Professor von Habert, would you like some coffee?"

"Excuse me, that's my secretary," the gentleman tells us.

The young woman in the white coat gives him a hand and she guides him towards the living room. "Are you looking for someone?" She glances back at us.

She sets the professor in a reading chair while she accompanies us to the head of the nursing home.

The heavier cases are housed one floor higher.

She referred to the floor as the camping department at Debenhams.

"It's not so bad. We have a lot of volunteers coming in. That's the advantage of a Protestant institution, eh?

"Father is not a Christian. He hates Churches."

Paul gives me a disapproving look. His eyes tell me to shut up.

"It doesn't matter, we accommodate everyone from all sects and denominations. We even have patients who are Masons and humanists. Even Muslims are welcome. This place is for everyone."

The phrase "even Muslims" puts me into thinking. I know what she means, but it seems like she is referring to criminals.

"But he does not go to Church. Is attendance mandatory?"

They laugh at me.

"We do not live in the Middle Ages!"

Someone in the corridor shouts: "Sister, Sister!"

The nun does not respond. The nurses rush to the hallway.

"Sister, Sister!"

I feel myself getting restless. It's a nagging, panicked call. Another volunteer rushes in. I assume that she is a volunteer, although it is hard to tell the difference.

"Someone has pooped in his bed and it smells like a cesspool!"

"I'm coming!" The nun calls out.

Sculpture

"Pressured?" I ask her.

"Too many patients, too few volunteers. Can you fill out the forms in the meantime?"

We fill in the needed forms.

We meet Professor von Habert again in the hallway. "Nice to meet you. I am the manager of this nursing home. Do you live here?"

Paul whispers: "Who would have thought that a good head would turn out to be a senile wretch?"

"But he is not that sick. He's healthy." I defend the old man.

"That's because he's senile. And that is harsh. But on the other hand, he might be happy now. Who knows, he might have been a wretched professor!"

"Then that would be good luck for him, right?" I tell Paul.

We enter the code and quickly open the door. The Professor wants to know the code, but we could not find him anywhere.

We sit on a happy terrace outside the demented building. I'm glad I'm out.

"It's all so sad," Paul remarked.

I see a lot of young people who waste their time drinking beer, smoking and laughing. They have a world of their own, but let them. They have the right to be merry.

Paul recently told me: "The present is the most important phase in your life. Now is all that matters. You do not have to worry about the future."

But I have my own concerns. I think about the afterlife and if it turns out that it is not true, then I realize that death is just plainly death.

"You have no other choice; this is by far the best option. You have to act fast- otherwise he will be on the waiting list.

The lists shows that he needs to wait at least half a year or one year to get inside the nursing home. Your mother will not come back just to take care of him. He'll be like Professor van Habert pretty soon!"

He's right. I am still single because my Dad does not want me to leave him in the lurch.

"Let me die first before you get married. But if you get married now, then you have killed your own father!"

A minute later he thinks that I am going to school.

We see a couple walking hand in hand ahead of us. He uses a cane so he can walk while she is almost blind that she cannot see where they are going. How long have they been together? I am now 25. I want to sell the parental home in Soest and I want to live in The Hague alone, without Father. I want to live my own life and freely practice my profession. I finished at the Academy and I want to use my degree to earn a living. I saw a beautiful, well-lit studio near Troelstrakade and I want to own it. I want to make myself immortal works of art. But the Japanese prisoner holds me captive. He has suffered so much and if Father does not go to the shelter, then I will not be able to fulfill my dreams. He needs to a place for refuge and I need a place where I can be free.

I suddenly realize that we have not seen Miss Paardekoper's sculpture. It is a large bronze statue with very thin legs and long arms. His open hands are on his forehead. The image is called *Forgotten*. I'm going back, I need to see it.

12

Father is not happy with the dog I brought home. I can keep my boyfriend with the snowball inside my bedroom but the dog needs to stay outside.

"Dogs belong outside," Father said. "Their mouth and their asses stink."

He had just woken up and he is still in his striped pajamas and thick terry robe. His hair peaks in all directions and he did not have his glasses on. He pokes his left pinkie in his ear and examines his finger. He repeats the action three times. Then he plunges his right pinkie on the other ear but it comes out empty. I hope he picks his nose too but my wish is in vain.

He is usually asleep when I go to school.

I think I'd better leave the dog inside the plastic bag and take him out when I get home from school. It looks like Father is in a bad mood and I do not want to make him angry so early in the morning.

I take Flip out the front door and place it beside the doormat so nobody could step on him. He is still small. I give him a pat on the head.

"Sweet Flip," I say.

"I do not want that thing on the front door!"

Father is right behind me. His morning breath stinks. He used to shower every day, but now he has changed.

"Put that bag of bones out the back door... I do not want to see him. You should be thankful that you get to keep him when I prefer to trample him like a cockroach. I hate clutter."

It's true. Everything in our home is neat and orderly. Even the forks and knives in the plastic tray should lie on a straight line in the appropriate box. If I accidentally bump into a chair and it moves a few inches out of line, Father puts it back in place. I am responsible for keeping everything spic and span-towels, teacups, coffee mugs, sugar jar and sprinkles. Dad tells me that he is teaching me to be tidy.

"I made the dog with Miss Paardekoper," I softly tell him.

"Well that makes it even worse!" He shouts.

He kicks the paper mache animal with his checkered slipper and it rolls over to its side.

"Miss Paardekoper likes him very much."

He angrily walks away from the door.

"Put that darn thing back where it came from or else I will throw that thing away!"

"Flip, you need to stay out back and maybe you will by the front door tomorrow."

I pick him up and pat him on his head. There is no shelter there and I hope that he stays dry.

I grab my backpack and walk out the door. Father is nowhere to be seen, he does not want me to say goodbye to him.

"Just go on your way," he tells me.

When I arrive, I see Tuyet running with Ada towards four other girls from our class. I pretend that I do not see them. But they rush towards me and encircle me. They point to my crazy long skirt and stupidly long stockings. I thought that they would just push me down but they have something else in mind. They notice my nose.

"Hey, I have a nose! Do you have a nose? That's funny because we all have noses but you don't."

Marijke pulls my nose.

"How strange, I don't feel anything."

She pulls harder.

"Let's see if we can pull it a little harder so it will be longer!"

Two girls simultaneously reach for my nose. Jane holds my head firmly in place and turns my head so I could face them.

"Hey, we are helping you out. You should at least be grateful."

They pinch my nose one by one. I hope that it won't bleed. Ada shoves me with her shoulder. I try to get to the entrance, but they block my way.

A girl is pulling at my skirt.

"What a silly low skirt!"

She pulls at my skirt and the other join in and they succeed at putting my skirt all the way down. I find myself in my underwear and my skirt is at my feet. They all laugh at me. Thankfully, I have clean underpants.

"Why did you call Tuyet a dirty gook?"

Ada shoves me a bit harder that I almost trip on my skirt. They push me from one side to the other and they pull at my backpack.

"I did not say that."

"Yes you did. Tuyet said so herself."

Tuyet does not say anything.

More kids crowd on me. I want to leave but I cannot get out of the circle. My skirt is now on the ground. A girl picks it up and hurls it away. I cover my underpants with my hands.

"Silence, you guys!"

She punches me on the face. My glasses fall at her feet. She kicks it and the other follow. When I bend down to pick up my glasses Henkjan pulls down my panty and squeezes my buttocks.

"She also has a dirty brown ass!" He laughs as he runs to the girls. My glasses are completely bent and the right lens is broken.

I wait for all of them to go inside the school so I can retrieve my skirt that is hanging on a branch. Fortunately, it is hanging from a low branch and I can just jump up and reach it. I quickly put my skirt back on and walk towards the school building. I hear the girls giggling at the end of the hall.

"A gypsy does not need glasses," Henkjan calls out. Everyone laughs at me. They call me a gypsy because I wear stupid clothes, black hair and have brown skin.

Tuyet takes a seat with someone else in the classroom.

I put my backpack on the floor and when I open it, I see the doll that Mom brought home as a souvenir. Mom bought it from a street child in India. It made from recycled materials. Mom told me that there are hundreds of street kids in India. The doll flies through the air in a flash as it passes from one child to another. It ends up with Ada just as Miss Vlasblom enters the classroom. Ada hides the doll in her bag.

"Tuyet, go and sit next to Lizzie."

Miss Vlasblom asked her nicely, but Tuyet wears an angry face and does not budge from her chair. The teacher walks up to her and I start to cry. I do not want to cry, but the tears came all of a sudden.

"Lizzie called Tuyet a dirty gook," Ada declares.

Ada has a big mouth. Everyone is afraid of her. The children around me chuckle. The teacher now looks at me and notices the broken glasses on the table.

"Lizzie, put your glasses on."

The class falls silent.

"It's broken," I tell my teacher.

"Put them on just the same." She instructs me.

I am embarrassed as I put the glasses on. I know that the children are laughing behind my back. The teacher looks around.

"How did you break your glasses?"

She looks at everyone.

"Good, I'll find out for myself."

Tuyet and I stay behind after class. The teacher wants to know what exactly happened. Ada looked at Tuyet just before she left the classroom and she shot her a warning look not to betray her or else she would be in trouble.

"Tuyet, I want to know what really happened." Miss Vlasblom said.

Tuyet starts to cry. Miss Vlasblom is leaning against her desk with her butt.

"I will not let you go unless you tell me the truth." She folds her arms across her chest to indicate that she is serious.

Tuyet tells the whole story starting from her visit at home and her encounter with Father. I liked her very much because all the others bullied me. But then Ada noticed that Tuyet accompanied me last Friday. The next day, Ada went to Tuyet's house and they became friends as long as Tuyet did not play with me. This morning, Ada waited for Tuyet and they walked to school together.

"And how did you break your glasses, Lizzie? I want to know the truth."

I am afraid that I will be bullied even more if I tell her what happened.

"It's just my nose," I make up an alibi. "It often falls because I have a stupid nose."

"No," Tuyet retorts. "Ada beat her."

Luckily, it rained in the afternoon. They are no longer waiting for us. We look through the window of the front door and do not see anyone. Maybe they are waiting for us in the shed by the gym. We are afraid to go outside. Miss Vlasblom walks up to us and opens her umbrella.

"Girls, I know that it is wet outside but I am certain that you will die from a little rain." She steps out and covers us with her huge parasol. She gets inside her car a few minutes later. The school yard is now empty. I hope that they have all gone home.

Tuyet and I walk together down the sidewalk hand in hand. We do not see or hear anything else except the pouring rain. We run down the street together and no one is around. We let go of each other's hand when we reach the next street and we run to our own houses. We are safely home!

I walk towards the back door and I do not see Flip anywhere. Miss Paardekoper told me that it must not get wet because it has not yet been sprayed with repellant. "Paper is fragile and you made a sensitive dog. You need to take care of him."

I think Father put Flip inside the house!

I see Father lying on the couch. I quietly walk inside the room, but I do not see him anywhere. I look for him in the hallway. I tiptoe towards my room.

"What do you want?" Father asks.

He just woke up from his afternoon nap and he is still in his pajamas.

"I am looking for Flip," I tell him.

"Who the hell is Flip?"

Flip is dead. Father threw him into the garbage.

"You call those wet newspapers a dog? Do you think I would want wet newspapers beside the back door?"

I start to cry.

"Go ahead and howl. That dumb dog is not worth a tear."

He is displeased that I do not have my glasses.

I take my snowball boyfriend in my lap as I sit on my bed. He can never take away my boyfriend. My boyfriend is dead.

13

"It's good that you are here with me, Father." I tell him. The nursing home does not suit him. He will surely die there. He may have Parkinson's disease even before he was in the nursing home or maybe it's a side effect from the anti psychotic drugs but he is now completely paralyzed. He does move anymore and he could not talk. His is as limp as a vegetable. His genius head has broken down. I do not know if ever studied Math, because I have never seen him in front of the computer. He used to go out during winter when it was still dark and he studied the night sky with his telescope. But he can no longer do that. His puzzles will remain unsolved.

Did he start his medication when he was a kid? He was thirteen years old when he was in the camp. He studied Mathematics in the Delft and I believe that he graduated with flying colors. Then he went with Mom to India for a few months. He did not want to leave her alone, all he wanted was to be with her. How long were they married? I think three years. But then things went wrong, and he fell into a depression. Miss Paardekoper said that he could not think of anything besides formulas. Mama gave up on him, and that was why she often went on tour. She could not bear to live with him any longer, but he still loved her.

I take him to my studio and put him in a well-lit corner. He sits on a wheelchair in front of a full-length mirror. Paul found the mirror in a flea market and he thought that I might need it. I want to immortalize Dad and I was inspired by Miss Paardekoper's nude self-portrait.

I want to make a life size portrait of Father in two feet by five feet canvas. I want to paint Father and his empty stare. His eyes see nothing, no past and no future. He is dead. He was the father I never liked, a figure imposed on me because I never had a mother. A father who preferred that he was dead rather than thankful that he was still alive, he had scarred my childhood as much as the Japanese have done to him. He was a father who was haunted by his own imagination while I fled in my own fairytale world. Do I owe him artistry if I remained as a child? Was I pleased with the adoption? I do not know. What if my childhood was different? Sometimes I get tired of all these questions and that is the reason why I chose him as my model. I want to remove him out of my system. I want to paint him out of my life so I could live an independent life. I have two fathers- one who sired me and the other who never cared for me. And, yes, I also have two mothers- the woman and the girl. I do not exactly know who gave birth to me and the mother who adopted me was never home. Who was I better off with? Not even one of them deserves me! The one only who truly loves me is Miss Paardekoper!

I glance over at Father and pity him. The man who could not give love, whose passion was stilled with Parkinson's will now be expressed in art. I render him and myself service as I paint him: He remains forever, I lose him forever.

I want a kid in the mirror to his left. I want to paint Father like a child in a stroller- hopeful and expectant. A cute kid-

75

playful, energetic, full of vitality and expression. Is there a child who does not want to be happy? Is there a child who does not have dreams? Is there a child who wished he was never born?

I want a monumental painting, a monument in oil. The playful child looks at the dead man. Is there a child who fears death? The child is excited about the future and open to anything that comes in his way. The dead man is a doll that the child can play with.

I make a rough sketch on the canvas with charcoal. I immediately fill it with thin, pure colors. The smell of turpentine fills the room, but Father remains silent. He is an ideal model. I now fill it in with white paint. It's crazy, but I love the man I am painting. I love his stern and disappointed face where all love, faith and hope is gone. Did the Japanese strip him of all those emotions? Wood thrown into the fire turns it into hoary, lifeless ash. But what if there is a lump of gold in that fire? Is the gold purer and more refined than before? Who determines what happens in your life and how you react?

I must be strong; I have to be nice to him. He cannot manipulate my life and he cannot ruin it. I do not want to be like him.

I paint his hands and they appear soft and warm like old men's hands with blue veins visible through the skin. I paint them soft, even if he has beaten me countless times. I am surprised that the pain he has caused me all these years begins to disappear as I paint him. I can actually paint the pain away! Father's image is increasingly pronounced on the canvas and the past slowly dissipates. Soon he is entirely transplanted to the canvas and out of my life.

His lips were once soft and full and he kissed Mom with tenderness even if I had not seen it. How could you paint a mouth that never uttered a word of understanding, a mouth that vomited wormwood for the last ten to fifteen years? I paint a bushy mustache over his mouth to conceal his condescending tone and cruel words forever. He often told me: "You belong to a madhouse." But his words will never hurt me again.

I had trouble with his eyes. He had that reproachful look because they had to take a child of the streets. He was disdained that they had to give a street kid a home when there are thousands of other children who suffered in the Japanese prison camp.

And his wife left him to travel the world, while he was stuck at home with a retarded child to care for. NO, he did not want that gypsy child.

"I'll paint it just the way they look. I have suffered enough."

I stayed, but Mom was always away.

I see the disgust in his eyes and I do not want to gaze at them ever again.

I walk over to him and put my sunglasses over his eyes. I cannot paint him with that stare.

Now I paint his wrinkles. The first one is between his eyes. One groove is deeper and longer than the other. What are they, Father? Where did the creases on your skin come from? Was it from the camp? Was it caused by a guard who shoved your face in the sand while another soldier put his boot on your neck to keep you from squirming? How long was your head buried in the sand? I remember that you were only thirteen.

Where did you get the strength to breathe, to survive? Why did you lose your life forever?

I make the wrinkles deeper and I soften the pains of the past.

The creases on his head crisscross each other as rivals. I have experienced a lot more than you.

I believe that I had caused at least one fold in his forehead because I was a difficult child.

I finally make his nose. I do not want it to be too small. I do not want anyone to laugh at him later.

I put my palette down for a while and take a seat.

Father's painting is almost done. He is alive, but he no longer lives in my blood.

I look at him and the painting. Then I walk over to him and naturally give him a kiss on the forehead. I have never kissed a guy before and this is my first time. He had tasted love before but he could not hold on to that love. He longed for tenderness, but he ended up in bitterness. "I understand, Father. I really do. I know that what you did to me caused you a lot of pain. You do not have to say it, Dad." I kiss him again, this time on the cheek.

A few moments later, I wake up in the stillness of snow. I had dozed off. A lot of snow has fallen and the bright light woke me up. The paint is still drying, and I see Father is still in his chair.

I turn the trolley towards the snow. The tires squeal, but Father remains silent.

"Everything is permanently covered with snow. Everything!"

I push the sliding doors and take him to the backyard. He still has the sunglasses and it protects his eyes from the light. I turn into a child once again as I lie on my back and watch the snow fall over me. I close my eyes and enjoy the moment. I throw handfuls of loose snow at Father. He's stuck in the cart and he does not budge. Did I see him smile for a moment? I am playing in the snow! I am playing with Dad in the snow! It seems surreal. It's as if the painting had changed our relationship. He no longer controls me and maybe, just maybe he is proud of himself and proud of my creation.

But I need to go back and finish the painting. I still need to paint the child.

I start to draw the child in Father's mirror. The newborn child is in the stroller. My child.

I fill it with paint, and give life to the child. I sigh as I draw the child's features. If I continue, the child will look like me and it could all go wrong. I see myself in the child and I cannot let that happen. He is not my real father, I am adopted. I recall my childhood with my hands. I crawl out of the trolley and paint.

How old was I when I went to India for the first time? Twelve? Thirteen?

My hands move on their own and paint a child leaning on a wall on the street, a child playing with a doll. She sits there alone. My hands start to shake, I cannot go on. This is not the monumental work that I had in mind. This is about Dad and maybe I should continue painting Father. But Father's image is already complete!

I put my coat on and walk out of my studio for a breath of fresh air. Father remains inside, he is safe and warm there. I wander aimlessly. Soon I reach park. I sit on a bench and try to relax. A child hops all the way towards me and sits beside me. She looks at me, and I want to hug her. I love this kid.

I make my way towards the studio and I see Farhad running towards me. He has a hat on. I do not recall if he had a hat before, but I recognize him from a distance. He has a thin mustache under his small nose. His eyes are happy. I rush into his arms, he holds me close and I start to cry. He strokes my back, looks at me and tells me: "I am so glad to see you again!"
Never before did someone yearn for me like he did.

14

I see mothers with very small children in the wide strip in the middle of the road. Some of the kids are asleep, deaf to the noise of passing cars, scooters, bicycles and carts. The road is broad enough for five cars. I see cyclists with huge loads attached to their bikes. It's amazing that they do not topple over. There are skinny, white cows in the middle of the road. The people ignore the cows and the cows in turn do not mind the traffic.

We walk past colorful shops that sell rugs, shawls, skirts, vegetables, fruits and spices. I can smell the red, yellow and ocher spices. It makes me happy. Women, men and children look pretty in plain white and multi-colored robes. There are more colors here than in The Netherlands. Is it because of the sun?

"See, Lizzie, there is nowhere else in the world that is more colorful than Delhi," Miss Paardekoper tells me.

Mom could not go with me to Delhi because she is in China for an important research.

"We have found wonderful bronze objects from the Han Dynasty," Mom says. "A bronze horse that is two thousand years old. I will tell you all about it when I get home."

She had bought the tickets long ago and since she cannot go, she asked Miss Paardekoper to accompany me instead. Father agreed with the arrangement. "Go ahead," he urged but I saw that it hurt him. Would he still love me?

I experience stomach pains. Miss Paardekoper thinks the tea caused it. She told me that you should never buy a drink from the streets because the water is not safe. I think it's not the tea that caused my tummy aches.

Tomorrow we will take a long taxi ride to visit an orphanage.

Children approach us and beg.

"You have to give them something," Miss Paardekoper tells me. "Otherwise more children will come to you. If you give money to them the older kids will use it to buy alcohol."

One of the girls is selling a wooden toy. She opens the box and there are small chess pieces inside. The box looks beautiful. I look into her eyes and she that her face is smeared with dirt. She looks like a gypsy. She looks like me.

Dad might enjoy this game, I think to myself. The girl tells me the price in perfect English: fifty rupees! I had calculated how much a hundred rupees would be in Dutch money and it was equivalent to twenty cents. So the wooden chess game costs ten cents.

But Mom reminded me that you should haggle so you would not get cheated.

I do not. What is ten cents when it can buy you a nice game of chess? I give her ten coins. She rejoices and gives me the box.

"How much did you pay for that?" Miss Paardekoper asks me. Fortunately she was busy looking at something else when I handed the girl the money.

"A dime," I reply.

"That's good a great deal, Lizzie. But you should haggle next time."

Suddenly twenty children come towards us with all kinds of stuff. Some do not have anything to offer, they just open their palms and ask for money. Their mothers are nearby and they also beg from the passerby.

"You do not need to buy anything; otherwise they will continue to come after us. It's sad that we cannot help all of them." Miss Paardekoper laments.

We continue to walk and I let the rupees fall from my hand. I look back and see the children scramble to pick up the coins.

We go inside a shop to ward them off.

I see thick gloves and hats with bright colors. It can get very cold at night during January, about seven degrees but the weather is usually warm in the morning. I think about the children. How do they keep warm? I want to buy a pair of gloves for each of them, but Miss Paardekoper tells me that it's impossible. There are millions of children who live on the streets and I cannot give all of them gloves.

We sleep in a fancy hotel behind the main road called Imperial Hotel. I have never seen anything so beautiful in my life. There are two people in nice uniforms that greet people when they enter the hotel. They always open the door for us and they greet us "good morning" or "good evening." The hall is way bigger than the one at home and it is very long. There are pretty pictures on the large columns in the middle of the hall. Miss Paardekoper tells me that she stayed in the hotel when she studied in India.

"We will also visit the National Museum in Delhi," she promised.

Our bedroom looks like a large living room with two large beds. There are two large chairs and a sofa and there are paintings on the walls. The bathroom is even bigger than our living room at home and they is a large bathtub where you can lie down and take a bath. I do not understand why so many

Ben Bouter

children sleep on the streets while I get to sleep in a soft bed in a nice hotel.

Miss Paardekoper and I have dinner before we sleep. We walk through a shiny corridor lined with tables with pictures and curved legs. There are paintings everywhere. The place is certainly for rich people.

There are huge chandeliers on the dining room and there are white signs on the tables with lots of glasses next to it. The chairs are all lined with white fabric that goes all the way to the floor.

I see a mad with a red jacket with gold buttons point to a table. There are Persian rugs on the floor and the tables are covered with a salmon-colored tablecloth. Once again, there are many paintings on the walls. The dining room is crowded with people dressed in nice clothes. Miss Paardekoper wears a long, black dress and I can see the top of her breasts. Her hair is tied in a pony tail as always and she looks like the Bollywood star being interviewed by a reporter on top of the stairs.

I am wearing a floral dress that Miss Paardekoper bought in a shop at the hotel. It fits me perfectly and I feel a bit posh. Two men in white suits pass by our table and give a friendly nod to Miss Paardekoper. She replies with a friendly hello.

"Great men are handsome," she tells me.

I feel honored as I sit beside her. If I go to Baarnsch Lyceum in September, I can tell my new classmates that I have been to a luxurious hotel in India. I hope that I will not be bullied in my new school.

"Do you like it here?" Miss Paardekoper asks.

I feel like I am in a movie set. I have never flown. We boarded a large KLM plane and we climbed the stairs to reach the upper deck where it is more spacious.

"Sweetheart, your mother loves luxury just like me. We make travel a party."

I get to choose what I will eat and drink and our chairs collapse into a bed. I watched movies on a screen next to my chair and I read books about India. I discover that India is a huge country with a population of one billion. The English were more dominant the Dutch who lived there.

I tell Miss Paardekoper that I think the place is nice, although I do not understand why there are so many poor children begging on the streets.

Miss Paardekoper sighs.

"Let's enjoy our fine dining, sweetie and we'll talk about it in the morning, okay? You'll see I have adopted a lot of them."

We eat Italian dishes- in India! I eat vegetables, fish and meat. I nibble at the dishes because I have never eaten it before.

"I stay here every time I am in India," Miss Paardekoper informs me. This is my favorite hotel. It has a bar filled with gorgeous men!" She laughs.

"So," she tells me when we are in our room. "You go to sleep. Tomorrow is going to be a tiring day. Do you mind if I go out for a drink?"

I lie on the bathtub as I listen to music from the speakers. Then I change into my striped pajamas and crawl on the big bed. I feel like a princess. Miss Paardekoper turns the light off on my side of the bed and she walks over to the mirror to check her outfit. She has changed into another long, black dress that makes her look beautiful and slender. I closed the zipper on the back of her dress and I saw the strap of her black bra. She is also wearing black pantyhose. Her lips are red and the beaded necklace on her neck is the same shade as her lipstick. It's half past nine in the evening and it is already dark. She has closed the curtains.

"You can read if you want, then you can turn off the light when you get sleepy. All right, Lizzie? You don't need to be afraid. I have stayed in this hotel and I have never experienced something bad during my stay. I will lock the door when I go out. Does that sound good?"

She walks back to the bathroom and she comes out with a sweet scent. She waves at me as she closes the door. I hear the lock turn and her delicious scent wafts in the air.

I read more about India and I learn about Hinduism. There are three hundred thirty million gods that depict the various characteristics of the same god. I soon understand that there are a lot of children on the streets because they are abused by their parents or step parents because they do not get enough money from begging or because their fathers are alcoholic.

I regret not giving more rupees to the girl who sold me the chess game. I think of them and where they might be sleeping when I am in a big bed in a fancy hotel. Why am I here while they sleep on the streets? Is that her reincarnation, her karma? Was she evil in her past life that she had to suffer poverty?

I feel my eyes are getting heavy and I turn off the light. It's already eleven o clock and it is very dark in the room. I lie on my back and I do not hear any sounds. It is very quiet. My leg twitches, a sign that I am about to fall asleep. I roll to my side and doze off.

I play with my colorful doll as I lean against a tree. My doll is alive. He often travels to distant lands but he always comes back to play with me. I do not any other kids, and he is my only friend. I just arrive because I fled from Aunt Nagalaskshmi who always hit me with her cane. I want to go to Mom and Dad, but they are no longer around. "Your parents are dead, and now I am stuck with you," Aunt Nagalaskshmi tells me. When she gets drunk, I run away and climb the back of a truck. Now I live on the streets and my doll is my only companion.

Someone is trying to get my doll. "He's mine!" I cry out loud but nothing comes out of my throat. I want to scream, but it seems that I have lost my voice.

I am afraid. I look around. Where am I? I do not recognize the shapes in the dark, not even my bed. Then I realize that I am in a hotel in Delhi. I had a very strange dream, a nightmare. I guess it's because of the book that I read earlier.

I turn on the light next to my bed and sit up. Miss Paardekoper is still out, and I am alone in the room. Something must have happened to her. I am afraid and so I leave the light on. I hear a strange sound, I think it's the air conditioning.

I want Miss Paardekoper by my side.

Do not cry, Lizzie. I tell myself. You're already twelve and you just had a bad dream about a sad, little girl. Dreams are illusions. The children on the streets frightened you.

I step out of bed and walk towards the bathroom. I turn on the light and I see my reflection on the three mirrors. The bathroom tiles are warm. There are white bathrobes that hang on hooks at the back of the door. One of them is just my size. I take it off the hook and put it on. I catch a sound, I hear something. I can look through the glass on the door but it is too high. I grab a chair, set it against the door and peek into the hallway. I see a long corridor with a lot of lights but I do not see anyone. Where could she be?

I slide the seat back and open the heavy door. I peer into the crack, but I see nothing. It's quiet. I leave the door ajar and step into the hallway. I hear a soft click. The door! My door! I walk back but I could not get it to open. I am stand alone, barefooted and dressed in a night gown in the empty corridor. I do not know what to do. I can sit down and wait for her at the door or I can look for her. She must be somewhere inside the hotel.

I walk into the hallway and pass an elevator. I see a big 4 next to the lift. Remember, Lizzie, 4. I walk past the elevator and into another hallway. I do not see anyone. It's late and I think that everyone is asleep. I am frantic.

I think that she's probably in the dining room downstairs. I walk back to the elevator and press a button. The lift appears a moment later. I step inside and I see a lot of buttons. I press 0, which is the ground floor, if I remember it correctly. I get out and see the large hall. There is a gentleman and a young lady is on his arm and they have their coats on. They are going outside. But it already late in the evening! I also see the two ushers by the door but they do not see me. I hear music coming from somewhere. Maybe Miss Paardekoper is in there.

I walk down the hall and meet one of the men that we saw in the restaurant. He speaks to me, but I do not understand him. He speaks English, a foreign language. I tell him in French that I do not understand him. He replies in English. I speak a little English and I tell him that I am looking for Miss Paardekoper. He takes my hand and tells me that he knows where she is and he will take me to her.

We go inside the elevator and stop at the third floor. We step in a corridor that resembles our hallway. We walk down and stop at a door marked 307. I try to remember the number. He inserts a card on the doorknob and it clicks open. He ushers me inside the room. The room is smaller than ours, but s nonetheless beautiful. The light is on and the bed looks like it's been slept in. I wonder why he is still awake. Older people sleep late and I do not know why they stay awake for so long.

He goes inside the bathroom and comes back a few moments later. He gestures to me to sit on the bed. I sit on the edge of the bed. I do not want to sleep here, I want Miss Paardekoper. He sits beside me as he lights up a cigarette. I move aside because I do not like the smoke.

"What's your name?" he asks.

I went with someone who does not even know my name. I should have stayed in my room. He stops me when I walk to the door. He tells me that I have to wait for Miss Paardekoper. I know the number of our room and Miss Paardekoper might be in our room and she will be worried sick if she finds out that I am gone. I want to leave.

The man in the white suit takes another puff from his cigarette and puts an arm around me. He rubs my cold feet and drapes a quilt over it to keep it warm. I think he is trying to tell me not to be afraid, but I am scared. I wished I never went with him. I thought that he was Miss Paardekoper's acquaintance because I saw they were cordial at each other over dinner.

He puts his ash tray down and stands up.

"Do you know what floor your room is?" he asks.

"Fourth floor," I mumble.

"How about the room number?"

I'm not sure if I should tell him.

"402, Right?" He wants me to confirm it.

It's true, I do not know how he could have known.

He walks over to the telephone beside his bed and dials a short number.

Who is calling in this hour? I hope he is not calling the police.

He talks fast and I do not hear what he is saying. Then he nods.

"She's coming," he tells me. "Miss Paardekoper is on her way."

I think he's lying.

He walks over to the mini bar, open a small bottle and pours the sparkling liquid in a glass.

"Here," he gestures. "You must be thirsty."

I do not understand his words, but I know exactly what he means.

I take a swig. It tastes sweet, and yummy. I almost finish the drink when I hear a soft knock on the door.

"Lizzie dear, I was so worried!"

Miss Paardekoper is in her dressing gown. Her hair is dripping. I think she just showered.

"Thank you, David," she says to the man. "Thank you for the wonderful evening. It was heavenly!"

She gives him a kiss and takes me back to our room.

15

Farhad is amazed that I have painted Father. He finds it an incredibly handsome portrait and an expressive painting. He does not know that Father has experienced a lot of hardships, but he can tell it with the painting. "I see a warm and cold man," he muses. He looks at the invalid man in the chair and the one in the canvas. "One is dead while the other lives!"

He removes his coat and cap. His curly jet black hair tumbles over his eyes.

He asks me: "Who is that cute kid?" as he drapes his coat on a chair.

I turn away and hide my face. I start towards the kitchen.

"Coffee?"

I cannot help but cry. The child in the painting evokes my childhood. All I had repressed and forgotten came rushing back when I was in an orphanage in Delhi and I unknowingly painted the kid on the monumental canvas. My hands moved independently from my head. It's as if I fell into a trance, it was a dream I had taken for granted and thought it was impossible. I was tired and confused and I do not know how long it took me to finish the child but I kept on painting. I had trouble with the child, but it turned out to be therapeutic for me. I was satisfied with myself when I was finished the portrait. It was an artwork of a man with a cruel and deformed past, along with a child who had no past. The child still had a future, but the man has nothing in store for him.

The head of the orphanage related how I was found. A nun carried me and she passed by a road where there were dozens of children led away to a labor camp run by cruel owners. I could not remember anything, except that I was playing with a doll. She told me that the Buddhist nun was unaware that she had walked into a place where kidnapping was rampant. The woman was on her way to the orphanage to protect me. Why was I protected? Did her religious garment shield me from the kidnappers?

I was taken care of and nourished in the shelter. According to Miss Paardekoper, Mom fell in love with me the minute she laid eyes on me and she did everything in her power to get me to The Netherlands. They had been married for ten years and they did not have a child of their own so they thought of adopting a child. Mom often said that adoption is a nobler cause than raising one's own child. It was years later when I finally understood what she meant.

Farhad runs to meet and I break into tears when he puts his arms around me. I weep for the child in the painting. The girl personifies so many children who are abused and raped across the world.

He turns around and presses his body against mine. I feel his warmth and his strength as he caresses my hair and kisses me. He has soft lips and a sweet mouth. He does not use his tongue to invade mine just like the other guys at the Academy did. I feel affection and warm connectedness in his embrace.

His hands slid over to my hips and my behind then he lets me go.

"Shall I make coffee?" He asks. "Sit down. Do you want white or black coffee?"

I believe I have found someone who is not just interested in having sex with me but someone who loves me deeply. But I do not know Farhad that well. If this is love at first sight, would it last long? For all I know, he might be using a famous tactic in India to lure women. How many women had he undressed? I sit on my chimney chair as I contemplate on my work. I often think of Miss Paardekoper as I sit on this chair. She is the one who saved my life. She is a powerful, headstrong and passionate woman who loves life and beauty and she has greatly influenced me. I will visit her soon. And when my relationship with Farhad deepens, I will introduce him to her. I want to know what she thinks of him.

Farhad and I stare at the canvas in silence. I love people who can be silent. Silent is often necessary. It can be wonderful. Silence is stillness; without words or music.

"What's your father like, Lalitha?"

He addresses me with my Indian name, my real name. Mom once called me Lalitha, which means elegant or beautiful. "But here we will call you Lizzie, "she immediately recants. "You are now in The Netherlands."

I lost my origins with my new name. My childhood was erased, it no longer exists. Perhaps it was too painful and even too sensitive to remember. Lizzie Backs, I was given Father's surname.

I had never realized that I was transformed so early in my life. I knew Mom meant well, and I think that a strange name gives rise to questions and ridicule. Lizzie Backs was a safe choice. Yet Lalitha slowly awakens, elegant but without a name.

"How did you know Lalitha was my real name?"

He smiles. "I know a lot more than you think."

He sounds rather familiar and mysterious at the same time. I do not probe any further.

Farhad can make good coffee. He even added milk that it tasted like cappuccino.

He even managed to find some cinnamon.

"But what I do not understand," he continues is why you walk around with the wheelchair with a doll that looks like your Dad. Did it ever occur to you that people might think you're crazy?"

He is the first person that bluntly states his observation. I know that it's crazy, but I made the wax figure myself. I made a mannequin in my Father's likeness. You might think that he is a fleeting image of someone at Madame Tussauds. I studied the wax figures all throughout my college internship. When you look at him longer, that's when you realize that he does not move and his expression remains unchanged. His hair was the hardest part to make.

I know that everyone enjoys the spectacle, some pity or even laugh behind my back. If there is anyone who is outspoken with his opinion, it's Farhad.

16

The first day after out trip, I wanted to change. I decided to be a hero. I want to be adventurous. I recently came from India and I've noticed that guys like me. They do not bully me, and they keep a respectful distance. I am an untouchable girl. I flirt and ignore them at the same time. I had learned this in India, and I will tell you more later on.

No one in my old school is in my class. Not even Tuyet. She went to Griftland College because that's what her aunt wants. We still see each other and we remain friends.

I think that the harassment is over. I hope so. The last time they bullied me was just before the holdays and before I went to India with Miss Paardekoper. I think Ada wanted revenge because Tuyet chose to side with me. After the swimming lessons, we were freely swimming in the pool when a number of girls pushed me under water. When I tried to swim back to the surface, one of the girls pulled at my legs. I was used to being harassed, but there were five of them and I could not breathe. I was constantly submerged as the girls held me and the boys grabbed my breasts and between my legs. I have never been so scared in my life thanks to a bunch of perverts.

I thought the horror was over and I swam my way to the stairs when two children jumped from the side of the pool and onto my back. I swallowed a mouthful of water and I could not breathe. I do not know who pulled my feet down and I could not get up. Images of Mom, Dad, the teachers,

Tuyet and Miss Paardekooper flashed before my eyes and they reached for me but I could not grasp. "Come here, Lizzie," Miss Paardekoper called to me, but she became increasingly blurred as I sank to the bottom of the pool. I was alone and I felt that I was sinking. I thought that it was the end and I was about to die. I thought that death was not bad at all and I was not afraid. No one can bully me anymore if I died. Everything around me went black and I felt like I was getting lighter and I was floating away. I saw a light around me and I saw the stars.

When I opened my eyes, I was on the edge of the pool and Tuyet told me that the lifeguard had revived me with mouth-to-mouth resuscitation. He was afraid that I was going to die because he could not feel my pulse. Everyone panicked. After three minutes, I was able to breathe again and I was taken to the hospital by an ambulance. Tuyet was one of the firsts to visit me in the hospital.

They took even took crazy pictures of my lungs.

The nurse said that Father could not come because he was not feeling well. I did not mind. I was actually pleased that he could not make it. I only wanted to see Mom and Miss Paardekoper. I was allowed to go home after two days and I never asked Mom what she told Father.

One time they locked me in the toilet after class. I felt so hurt that I grabbed my coat. I was afraid that they would take my coat again and throw it high up in a tree. I ran and hid in the bathroom. I peed and when I turned the doorknob, I realized that it was locked. I could hear them laughing behind the door and then they all ran away.

At first I did not know that they had locked the door. I tried to open the door, but it wouldn't budge. I did not dare call for help, because I knew that they were blocking the door and they would beat me up if someone helped me get out. One time I had to hide behind a tree for an hour just to wait for all of the kids to go home.

The lights on the hallway and in the bathroom went out. It was already dark outside. It was a Friday, and I was left alone and I was afraid. Father might not notice that I was still not home and Tuyet did not come to school that day because she was sick. No one would miss me. It was the weekend, and the school was closed until Sunday.

I looked at the window high above the toilet. It opened and closed with a bar, but I could climb all the way up because the wall was slippery. I tried to climb on the toilet and walk along the rod, but I was afraid that the rod would break. I sank back to the toilet sit to think. I felt humiliated, but I stayed still. Father might notice that I was missing when he would go to bed. I did not have a watch and I did not know what time it was.

I do not know how long I sat there, when suddenly I heard someone walking a dog near the toilets at the back of the building. "Help!" I cried out.

"Hello, is anyone there?"

It was a chirpy woman's voice. She told me that she would call the police and after a while I heard voices. The cleaners came along with the police. The agents took me home and that angered Father. He thought that it was stupid that I got locked inside the toilet.

"Well you certainly made a fool of yourself. It serves you right." He told me.

I am now studying in Baarnsch Lyceum and things are better. I feel a lot more confident after my trip with Miss

Ben Bouter

Paardekoper. Why should I complain? I may even have a brother who lives on the street, or maybe he is a labor camp. Do I even have a brother? There are millions of children on the streets, or in prison, who are abused and maltreated. I talked to guys who cleaned the sewers for a living until they were adopted by a charitable institution. They were nine girls who were forced to work as maids and they were not allowed to go to school. They were beaten and raped. Me, I was merely bullied.

They no longer call me Lizzie. I am now Lalitha Backs. I know it sounds really hot, but I want to change my name to Lalitha Paardekoper, and that will be the most beautiful name I could ever imagine.

I met young women from a higher caste while we were in the hotel. They had light brown skin. In Holland, I had brown skin, but in India I was surprisingly whiter than most people. The whiter the skin, the better. The young women wore saris made from the finest fabrics and they were tastefully modest in their dress. They were chic and restrained, confident but not arrogant. Western men treated them with respect. I saw that the men admired their beauty from a distance and they were strikingly different from the women who peddled themselves. I realized that I wanted to be just like these refined young women. I'm going to a new school and I will exude dignity and I will gain respect in return.

I try to talk to Father and ask him about the photographs that captured their visit in India. He had his hair combed back and he had a thin mustache like he did in Miss Paardekoper's painting. He seemed happy back then. I saw pictures of Mom and Dad with other men and women. Was that taken in Delhi?

98

The women had large, dark eyes, beautiful mouth and a small nose. They feel like family.

I wondered if Mom and Dad stayed in a hotel or did they rent an apartment in the three months that they were in India. I have never given it much thought until my visit. I smelled the scents and I had to know more. Do Mother and Father know where I come from?

17

Father is extremely cheerful today. Miss Paardekoper has invited him for lunch. This afternoon I will be at Grandma Moes, behind the petrol station on Church Street. I am glad that Father is out of the house and that Miss Paardekoper has asked him for lunch. Maybe she in painting him another portrait or maybe they want to talk about our recent trip to India.

I show Dad a picture where he and Mom are together with a man, a woman and a young girl about nineteen.

"They are beautiful people. Who are they, Father?"

"Those pictures don't matter anymore. It means nothing."

He walks away as I turn the page of the photo album.

"I have to get ready, otherwise I will be late."

A few minutes later, he comes back down. I can smell his Tabac cologne. He has shaved off his mustache and his lips are in a straight line instead of the usual pout. He probably ironed his own shirt because it looks wrinkle free. I have not seen him as elegant for months. He had combed his wet gray hair back. He even cleaned the living room. Miss Paardekoper's house is only fifteen minutes away, ten if Father walks briskly.

The dining table and chairs are aligned, as they have always been. The armchair is leveled with the road so he can see the postman and if he is getting mail. There is a freshly washed, crocheted doily where props his head when he sleeps. Even the dishes in the cupboard have been dusted and they shine behind the polished glass. Father was busy cleaning the house these past days. It's as if the invitation breathed new life into him. I have never seen him so enthusiastic, not even when Mom came home after her trip.

I have done my part too; I cleaned the windows and washed the dishes. I also did some vacuuming. Father has not cooked for some time, he lets the farmer deliver pizza or if he wants something else, he sends me to the Chinese restaurant for takeout. We warm the soup and eat from the can. I get to eat bread the entire week because we store it in the freezer so it will not get stale. Father writes his grocery list in a notepad and if I get a deficit, I have to pay it straight from my piggy bank. I get Fifty Guilders a week, but sometimes Mom gives me a few more when Father is not looking.

I end my probing and put the album away. I do not want to spoil his day. He had not been angry at me for the past few days and I only had to go to my bedroom once when I arrived home nine minutes late because the children hid my bag. But Father tells me that it's my fault.

He still has an hour to spare, but he has already finished his chores. He impatiently walks through the room and up the stairs. He needs to be busy to pass the time away. I smell his aftershave as he walks up the stairs. He sits down and looks at his watch and checks his shoes. He breaks off a shoelace and I need to quickly get a replacement from the store. He gives me the broken piece and he sends me off to the store. As soon as I enter the store, I realize that I had forgotten to ask for money, and I did not have anything to pay for my purchase.

"Never mind," the old boss tells me. "You can pay for it next time."

He gives me a wink before I go. I dash towards the house. I cannot keep him waiting.

"What took you so long?" he impatiently asks.

I back away from him. I think he is nervous.

I open the photo album once he's gone. It strikes me that there are a lot of pictures of the same family. They might have been my parent's good friends while they were in India. Maybe Grandma Moes can tell me more about then.

Grandma Moes lives just right behind us, down the street and around the corner. I think she's nice, but you never know where her hat stands. She lives alone because Grandpa died a long time ago. Her hair is always in a net so it won't fall on her face. She is very neat, much like Father. I always take off my shoes when I enter her house. I put on thick socks because it's a little cold but the weather is still nice nonetheless. I walk past the walled garden and down the steps. Father lets me play in the garden when he wants to talk to Grandmother when he is bored and he no one to talk with because Mom is always away. Mom thinks that Grandma is a whiner, but Father send me over and I even stay with her for a week.

I walk toward the garden doors and peek inside. I cannot see all the way through because the garden is reflected on the window.

Normally Grandma Moes sits by the window. I walk to the back door and I am lucky that it is open. I take my shoes off and quickly walk across the granite floor towards the kitchen. I do not see her. There is nothing on the stove, and I do not see any dirty dishes in the plastic bin. But I hear the refrigerator humming and I smell that the litter box stinks. I walk down the hallway and knock on the door of the drawing room.

"Grandma, it's me. Lizzie."

I softly tap on the door. I do not want to frighten her. I do not hear a response. I carefully push the door open and tiptoe inside.

"Do not make a mess on the window with your dirty fingers. I just washed them."

She's home. I shake her hand.

"What do I get?" I curtsy at her.

"Well, you do not have to. Forget about decency. Did your father send you?"

"No, I want to pay you a visit by myself." I tell her.

"What, now you're lying? I was supposed to give you Guilders because you're going to a new school but you can forget about it. Children who lie do not get rewarded. Why is he not here?"

"Father is at Miss Paardekoper's. She invited him to lunch."

"Was he the only guest?" Grandma Moes was suspicious.

"I do not know if she had other guests. Father did not tell me anything." I informed her.

"No, I guess not. It seems Sodom and Gomorrah did. I know those so-called artists. You're father must be crazy. I've done my job and I raised him well. Now leave me alone."

I walk up to her and give her a kiss but she waves me off.

"I do not have anything to do with ass-kissing. Tell your father that I had raised him otherwise than that. Now, get out."

She did not raise him. I know that she is his stepmother.

"Have a nice day, Grandma! I call out as I gently close the door. I am free at last.

18

"We can bring Father back home," I tell Farhad. "I have not visited him for a long time. I just can't see him."

Farhad is the first man to cook for me. Back when I was a student, men brought over pizza or Chinese takeout and if they were diligent, sushi from a far away Japanese deli. I think they all had one thing in mind: sleep with you. Not that I really liked it, but it was the clumsy and uncomplicated culture at the Academy. I enjoyed countless conversations about life, beauty and passions. Sex was an obvious dessert, it was a natural as brushing your teeth before bed. For me, it was a wonderful time, a time of discovery away from home, amidst people with a different perspective about life.

Now we talk about love, care and attention. He makes time for me and he is very commited.

He makes the *thalis* on a flat metal plate and vicariously prepares bowls of rice, yogurt, a special kind of bread, fried crackers with lentil flour and a large plate of chutney.

"I have also added in tamarind, ginger, mustard, garlic, pepper, onion, coriander, cumin and lemon juice," Farhad explains to me as he sets the chutney on the table. "And sugar, lots of sugar for a sweet girl."

He had picked me up this morning. I expected a big, flashy car but he came with an ugly, bright yellow duck. He looked fresh and tastefully dressed. I admire him for not following the fashion trends. I regard people who have their own sense of identity, who want to stand out above the rest. He loves clothes and he buys his own clothes. Who doesn't love clothes?

"We're going to my house," he informs that he has thought of buying a house. "It's a house that I like although it's not too big."

His eyes are dark, but not almond shaped like most Indians. There is a sloping roof on top of his eyelids and it gives his eyes a warmer and friendlier look. I feel calm and confident when he is around. I love to lie down on his rock hard chest.

Farhad studied Architecture in The Netherlands and he has now crossed over to real estate. He first worked as an adviser to a trader and when he saw how fast and easy it was to make money from building and selling properties, he started his own business.

He tells me that he comes from a wealthy Indian family and I believe him. He has breeding and that can only come from a noble lineage.

We drive through The Hague and go on the highway towards Rotterdam.

"I thought you lived in The Hague?" I asked.

"Just because I have a few small buildings in that place doesn't mean that I live there. But you're right, I used to live in The Hague, Loosduinen to be exact, close to the lips of the sea but the properties were not marketable so we renovated and sold it for double the price to an Indian diplomat. Relationship are as valuable as gold."

He explains in a matter-of-fact way that I do not detect a boastful or luxuriant attitude. I was quite suspicious.

It's a boring stretch between The Hague and Rotterdam. The highway is merely functional; there is no joy or grandeur on the road.

Farhad's fingers are bare and he does not have any ring. I do not know anything about watches, but I am relieved that he is wearing a simple timepiece with red leather. He does not have a thick gold chain on his neck and he does not wear a bracelet on his wrist. Is my perception of real estate guys twisted or is Farhad just an exception? There is nothing tacky about him.

"Do you like it that you are in the company of a stranger or are you scared?"

He is certainly not a stranger. I know him. I think it stems from the fact that we share the same background, same culture and ethnicity.

"I now live in one of the oldest houses in Rotterdam. You'll love it."

I am not familiar with Rotterdam. The only place I've been in that area is the Museum of Agriculture and Ethnology. I visited the museum together with Miss Paardekoper in preparation for our trip to India. I was a child back then and I finally understood why Mom worked as an archaeologist in India and China. Who would not be fascinated by the graceful images such as the *dancing bronze girl* from the Mohenjodaro area, which is now present-day Pakistan? I was also impressed by the stunning bronze female figure of the oldest civilization in that area, the Mehr Garth. The figure had a narrow waist and a heart-shaped torso with two strong, round breasts. "We are nothing compared to this,Lizzie." Miss Paardekoper said.

It's crazy, but Eva was always Miss Paardekoper while she always called me Lizzie.

I saw many quirky and twisted images of women during that era. It could easily pass as modern art though it dates back as early as 3000 BC or even earlier. How did they pass the craft from father to son?

"We're going to visit more often, sweetheart. I find the art of antiquity inspire the art of today," Eva told me.

But we never went back.

Farhad drives his yellow duck on the Coolsingel. He stops for pedestrians.

"You're not going to Scheepvaartkwartier, are you?" I ask him.

"Why not? This is one of the most beautiful areas of the city. I have nothing against Rotterdam, but this neighborhood exudes history. They will soon build a new bridge over the Meuse, near here. I've seen a number of designs, including an elegant swan. Can you imagine an elegant swan that can transport people from one side of the Meuse to the other? I would love to drive my duck on the swan!"

He turns left on Westerkade and parks his car on Zeemenstraat.

We stand in front of a sleek and stark building. I cannot imagine that he owns it. How old was he again?

"This boy owns the ground floor and the three top floors." He tells me. "You don't believe me, do you? You can stay here if you want, it's very spacious!"

He leads me into a narrow hall with marble floor.

"Let's go straight to the first floor. I use the ground floor for storage."

We walk up the elegant stairwell and we enter a huge suite. There are striking large windows and there are two fireplaces made from black marble. The walls are entirely white. There are wonderful modern and classical paintings next to each other on the walls. I look at the ornaments on the ceiling.

"This is a national monument," Farhad tells me. "We restore it as much as possible in its original state. Did you know that it was a pawnshop in 1875?"

The second and the third floor have similar rooms and baths.

"What do you think?" Farhad asks me as he points to the front room on the second floor. "I mean, can this be a studio?"

I see two huge windows that are five feet long and just as deep. The lighting is breath-taking. It's crazy but I think that the space is indeed perfect for a studio. But where will I place my bed our bed?

I feel happy and confused at the same time. Everything is happening so fast. That's not good.

The back room serves as his bedroom. It is very spacious and there is a fireplace as an accessory that is apparently not used. He had a nicely-formatted double bed. Does he own a colorful duvet as well? Or is this a woman's touch? I dread the idea that he might be gay.

"I've never slept here with a woman before," he says softly.

Not here, I think. But why a double bed? Instead, I blurt out: "But I see a woman in this house."

"Because it's tasteful? Hey, I studied architecture and I added two more years of interior design. I expected that an artist would not be prejudiced."

He grabs me by the shoulders and pulls me towards him. He smells nice.

That was just this morning. We are now sitting on the table enjoying Indian food, complete with all the colors and the spices.

"I'm going to check out the property in Delft," Farhad informs me as he thoughtfully chews on his food. I see a man who is used to eating in posh company and he does not show any male indifference. I do not miss the bravado, but it makes me a little suspicious. I do not trust people. I think that something is not right. This is our fourth date. His visit to my studio was the second meeting, while he called me for a third date. He was always courteous and he always showered me with attention yet he had tried to seduce me. He previously held the boat and I was prepared to go much farther. But all he did was hug me, give a sweet kiss and lovingly rub my back. There was nothing else after that. Maybe I was disappointed, but I was not fond of guys who wanted to jump right in and have sex either. Sex for me was linked with trust and with love, you can even call it affection. I am much stricter than I was in my student days. I have been celibate for a number of years and I want to save it as a gift for the man whom I will marry.

"The father of one of my friends wanted to buy this house," he continued, "and asked me to inspect it and give him a thorough report. It's crazy, I felt right at home. The whole Scheepvaartkwartier was designed by Architect Rose in 1840 for a rich banker and wealthy coal merchant Van Beuningen. Marten Mees was one of the bankers who moved into the building and this property is now a national monument among hundreds of buildings in The Netherlands. Did you know that this was spared during the WWII? I love buildings with a rich history."

He leans over to me and softly whispers: "And same thing goes for gorgeous women with a history."

We silently sit for a minute; words are not needed as the silence fills in the strain.

"But let me go back to my previous question. Why did say that you cannot let you father go? What is between you and your father?"

I said I could not. And I meant it.

"My Father is the man who married my mother. He wanted my mother, but did want anything to do with me. I was adopted, Farhad. He was stuck with me and I with him. We had to put up with the arrangement while Mom was away. He hated me and I do not know if the Japanese camp broke him or if I made him crazy or both, I do not know. But I am glad that he soon became senile and I could finally put him away. I thought I could get rid of him just as easily but he stayed with me even if he was in Scheidam and I was in Soest. I still felt his presence even if he was far away. I missed his cynicism, his sadness, his humiliating harassment. I suffered from his cruelty even if I had moved to The Hague. He haunted me when I looked in the mirror. He scorned me when I made an image.

You're too stupid, you cannot do anything. You are a stupid and ugly child. I never liked you. I heard his words over and over. I destroyed all my beautiful creations because his commentary made me crazy.

Miss Paardekoper sent me to Paul, a therapist and after a series of conversations he came up with the idea that I could paint Father. Maybe if I could paint him I could gain an understanding of my emotions and the pain would wither away. He would in turn, disappear from my life. I know it sounds absurd, but I felt the pain drain away when I painted him. Each stroke released me from his cruelty. Surprisingly, I felt lighter. I soon rid him out of my system and I transposed him into a painting. Tomorrow I'm going home to fix everything. I will go and see him, really. I will take him out on the wheelchair and see how he reacts. He is the person that he is and I now have a personality and a life that I can call my own."

19

"I cannot stay longer, Lizzie."

Mom is home for an entire week to regulate business. I hoped that we could do some things together while she is here but she has so many things to do with so little time.

"Sweetheart, I'm going back to China really soon. I still have a lot of work to do. Here, take a look at this." She grabs a pile of pictures from her purse.

"They have discovered the mausoleum of China's first emperor, Lizzie. I am going there to examine it along with a number of archaeologists. I'm talking about a historical find more than two hundred years before Christ. Can you imagine it, Lizzie? Two hundred years before the Western world was fascinated with the carpenter from Nazareth, there was already an emperor in China. I dug out the emperor. I looked into his kitchen cabinets and his bedroom. We will publish all his well-kept secrets. Do you understand how special this is? It is like the first chair that Jesus made. I discovered his sandals in the clay and the cup he used to sip his wine. That's how important this find is.

The whole site is two and a half square kilometers and there were temples and government buildings that were unearthed. This is an entire underground world! Mommy needs to help uncover these important artifacts. It's really important. You know what? Last month, we discovered a burial pit with beautiful bronze sculptures of birds and horses. Look"

She shows me a picture.

"You have to know history and I am glad that I can contribute to it. As such, Mommy needs to return to China. You will understand everything when you get older." She tries to convince me that she is needed in China.

"How long will you be away?" I ask her.

I see the horses, birds and charioteers. They look well-made, but I do not care. I see pictures of skeletons of young people. Human sacrifice. The laborers were sacrificed when they were no longer able to work. Tens and thousands were buried alive.

I think of the Indian orphanage where Mom found me.

"I need to be away for a long time, baby."

She pulls me close, pressing my head against her chest as she rocks back and forth.

She always leaves, but they never come back. The children who were sacrificed in the underground city were more important than me. I feel like I'm choking. She pulled me out of India to and buried me alive with a crazy father in one coffin.

"I do not want you to leave," I plead with her. "I do not want to stay alone with Father."

"Darling, I do not love him anymore and we have settled this before. You need to stay here and everything will turn out fine, you'll see." She strokes my hair.

"Look, honey." She says out of the blue. "Look."

She points to a pyramid.

"Mommy is busy unearthing the first emperor of China. History is exposed. I believe that he was thirteen years old when he succeeded his father; just a little younger that you, Lizzie. He did not have a father and his mother was the only one who lived with him. Soon he started building the Great

Wall of China, the longest wall in the world and he founded a city and he was buried in it so that he would remain immortal. She pointed to the photos on the table.

"He united the warring clans together and he made a great nation. Now we are investigating his hidden city. The emperor wanted to be immortal and he hoped that the city he buried with him would remain a secret. It was paradise with mercury rivers. People who built the city were buried with him so that his secret would remain safe. It is very interesting that there were many young people who were buried alive. We want to know what they ate, what diseases they had, there is so much more than we can discover. This exploration is going to take years, even decades. That is why Mommy needs to stay in China. But I'm going sure that you will come to China when you finish school. In three years' time you will be able to fly to China. Would you like that?"

She keeps the photos, satisfied with her explanation. Mommy thinks that the problem is solved. She has not used the word "never" but now she is leaving us for good.

I have to endure Dad for a few more years then I can go to China and join her.

Mommy and mummy, I now realize that there's hardly any difference between these words. I wish I was dead like a mummy.

"You can stay with Miss Paardekoper if you want. I talked to her and she promised that it won't be a problem."

Now Mom is gone and Father shuffles to put everything back into place: towels, tea towels, dish cloths, the stuff in the shower, toothbrush, toothpaste, everything. Father washes the windows while I vacuum under the couch. He checks to make sure that I had cleaned it thoroughly.

"This will not do," He lifts the bank side and there's still dust all right. We drink tea afterwards. I look at the farm across the road and see that there are many streaks on the window.

"And now we are going to take a shower," Father declares. "We will wash away your Mother's smell and we will begin a new era."

I clean up after he finished taking a shower. The shower gel needs to be just at the edge, next to the soap dish and the plastic curtain must be drawn away neatly. At the corner of the mirror is his favorite cologne, *Tabac*. I was afraid that it would break when I knocked it over once. It has to be in the exact same place and the brand must be visible.

"You're not going to stay with Miss Paardekoper," he yells from the top of the stairs. "I'm the boss around here and I am going to run this household whether you like it or not. From now on we will grow our own vegetables and we will only eat Dutch food. No more take outs. You cook and I take care of the garden."

It's been a long time since Father had said so much. He does not sound bad, it think he was relieved at the most. Father has once again glimpsed at the future. I think that he is just like a car window whose view was obstructed by the rain but the wiper removes it and a wider perspective appears. He hopes that I will be the wiper.

I want to read before I go to bed. Father never reads. I want him to read to me and I walk up to him and sit on his lap. I am now fourteen and this is the first time that I sat on his lap. He has strong legs and hard knees. He is reading a book about India that I have never seen before.

"I should have never left," He tells me. "Never."

"Why not, Father?" I ask him cautiously. This could be the only chance that he would open up about himself and India.

"Because it was the only love that I have ever known."

He was startled with his own comment.

"Lizzie, it's bedtime. What are you still doing here?"

He pushes me off his lap.

"Go and brush your teeth real quick."

I cannot sleep. I think of the men, women and children who were buried alive because the Emperor did not want anyone to find his grave. Now Mom has found it! They scoop out the sand and throw it at me. I am still alive, but they will lock me up in pit full of sand. I think I am going to paint pictures of children buried in the sand. I will make it so realistic that people will think that they are alive and maybe they will live again!

It's very dark and quiet. I hear the sound of a shovel as it lifts off sand and I see fine, light brown particles thrown at me. It lands on my feet then to my legs and on my stomach. I try to squirm but my hands and my feet are stuck and they are encased in stone. I try to scream as the sand gets on my head but no one can hear me. I close my eyes otherwise the sand will enter my eyes. You will unearthed after thousands of years, Lizzie and everyone will know that your Father and Mother buried you alive.

I am startled when I hear Father's voice. It's time to get up. Father opens the curtains. He is already dressed.

"Take a shower," he orders. "I made you breakfast and you are still in bed."

There is a towel in a shower and it is still wet from Father's shower. The water falls on my body and washes away all the sand. I use the shower gel that smells like roses.

When I come down to the kitchen, the table is already made.

"We eat together," Father tells me. "Here's you tea. Lime blossom tea. Do you like it?"

I do not recall eating breakfast with him. There are two place mats on the plastic table and the bread is a scale and not in a plastic bag. Jam, chocolate sprinkles, eggs in cups with white dots and slices of liverwurst stand in a straight line between us. There is a fork on the left side of the plate and a knife on the right; the utensils are exactly the same height. Father has combed his hair back just like he did whenever he went to Miss Paardekoper.

"Lizzie, do you have a test today?"

"What did you say?" I could not believe what I was hearing.

"I asked you whether you have a test today. School is almost over, so I presume that you are about to take your final exams."

How long has been since he had asked? He never bothered to look at my report card. It was Miss Paardekoper who signed it.

"I have one last test tomorrow, mathematics."

"I can help you if you want, Math is my specialty." He offers.

Mom's departure has made a miracle! I thought that I had to live in a madhouse for a few years but it seems like the Emperor has risen!

I ride my bike to school with a big smile on my face. I sing a song I used to hate out of sheer joy. I use my bell as my guide. People will think that I am crazy. I purposely take the route along the Peter and Paul Church which was built in 1350 according to Mom. There are dozens of people buried under the Baron Snouckaert of Schauburg. I had to repeat the name a few times so I could get it right when Mom and I visited the Church.

"Come on," she invited me. "We are going to look at the grave of Baron Snouckaert of Schauburg with ou, au and ae. The man will be happy with his tombstone because the Lord will not even remember his name."

We always laugh at that joke.

"Hello, Henry Philip, Baron Snoukaert of Schauburg," I cry out loud as I pass by the Church. An old lady glares at me. Was she a descendant? According to the tombstone, the man lived a hundred and twelve years and I imagine that he must've been deaf when he died. I make crazy turns with my bike and I even scream louder when I bike inside the tunnel. The man working in the garden of the second house past the tunnel laughs at me.

"You're elated," Miss Blankerstein noticed. She is about fifty and still single. She teaches English and I am good at English. She makes English fun and easy. There are other teachers who make sure that you do not understand the lesson, but not her. Everyone respects her. She is strict, but in a nice way. She has the face of a peasant woman, but when she speaks in English she is majestic. During our first lesson, she asked a boy to read the text 'they are' and he pronounced it as 'see ar'.

"Jos, the sea is in Scheveningen." She immediately said. "You roll the tip of your tongue against the back of your upper teeth and that might be a problem."

His teeth were far too forward. She immediately apologized to the boy. "I am sorry Jos, I apologize. What I said was rude." No one knew what she meant with the phrase. Jos had braces a week later.

I was happy when I was in school. I was glad that I was away from home. Holidays were the hardest. It was long and dreary and I was never allowed to go someplace else. The only exception was when I was in elementary school. I liked learning, it was fun. I could get along with anyone. I was not interested in boys, I found them childish and rough. The only person I cared about was my Physics teacher. He was not only young, but has the suave of an artist and the wit of Socrates. He was a good teacher. He explained difficult concepts well that they seem pretty easy to follow and understand. He suddenly confronted you with a question.

"You, Luca. Why does lemonade go up the straw if you suck it?"

No one had an immediate answer.

"Emma, you have a straw inside a glass of lemonade. How high does the lemonade get inside the straw?"

"It's the same height as the straw," the student replied.

"Fine. But why does the lemonade increase when you suck at the straw" Answer the question, Dimitri."

"Because the lemonade has a crush on me!"

The whole class laughs, including our Physics teacher.

"You, Lizzie. What's the real answer?"

I have no idea. Nobody knew the answer.

"Because of my appeal," I finally said. Chuckles fill the classroom.

"If I had a glass of lemonade, I would take out the straw." He told the class.

I was in love. The explanation that the air pressure drops in the straw because you suck the air and the law of atmospheric pressure was lost. Some other natural phenomenon occurred to me: butterflies in my stomach.

I felt a bit tense as I bike home. I hope that the atmosphere remains unchanged. I cannot believe that Father is now a real father after all these years. I cycle with Fleur and a bunch of girls along Stadhouderslaan. Iris turns left at Short Brinkweg and Iris takes the tunnel on the Great Melmweg while I go straight to the Long Brinkweg. I pass Middelwijkstraat and go around Kerkpad and reach Ferdinand Huyck. I stop by Miss Paardekoper who lives on the corner of Peter van den Breemerweeg. I want to extend my dreams as far as my route. When I want to delay time, I take the path at Soest: church, bakery, past the small buildings at Anton Pieck and across the wide pastures.

I reach Peter van den Breemerweg and I see dad emerge from Miss Paardekoper's house. She waves at him as he walks toward our house. I stop by and put my bike on my one side when Father has walked further down the road. I ring the bell. I see the beautiful floor of the hall; I always get the feeling that I am in a big chess board because of the black and white tiles. It gives the house a stately aura and I feel rich as I enter the hall.

"Your father was just here." Miss Paardekoper tells me.

"Oh!" I pretend that I did see him leave.

"Did you not see him? He left just a few minutes ago."

She walks straight into the studio at the back of the house.

"We talked about our trip to India and he reminisced about the time he visited the place. Did he ever tell you that he was head over heels in love while they were in India? But that would not many sense because now your Mother is in China and they are finally getting a divorce! Do you want something to drink?"

Mom and Dad are getting divorced! I knew what was coming: bad temper loomed in the horizon.

"Cola? Do you have cola? Get me Pepsi, Pepsi Cola." I replied.

I hear her pour two glasses.

"Your father was very excited," she announced as she walks over with the glasses.

I plop down on the couch. I do not understand why they need a divorce. They were already separated; they rarely saw each other and lived separately. I rarely see them talk to each other. What happens to me if they get a divorce? Will I still be able to go to China? How long do I need to stay with Father?

"The separation will do you all good. You're old enough to understand and I see that the heavy weight has been lifted off his shoulders. That woman from India stood between your Father and your Mother. If only she did not neglect your Father those three months they were in India... She was so busy that she never bothered to entertain him. She was always obsessed with old junk and a shovel. She was always on her knees digging for the past but never an eye for the present. No, offense but your mother is a good friend of mine. I often told her that she is digging her own pit, but she lectures me that the past heralds the present and without history, there would be no future. Her gaze was always downward; she was like a mole that despised daylight. Archaeologists get blind, eventually. But your father... He was so in love with I suppose a gorgeous young woman... Oh, the drama!"

I take a sip. Pepsi tastes better than coke.

"So, there you go. I understand that your father wanted to talk about it and now he wants me to paint the woman he fell in love with."

She stands up and walks over to the table filled with tubes of oil paint. She paints in one corner and sculpts in the other. She takes and few pictures and hands them to me. They were pictures of a beautiful Indian woman with brown skin and dark eyes. I recognized her from the photos we had at home, she often posed beside Mom and Dad.

"Pretty woman," I remark.

"Well, that surely explains why your father fell in love with her. Look at her lips, and those eyes that long for love, for attention. But he was married and she was stuck on a dead end street. It just wouldn't work. But he never forgot. I do not even know if she was nice to him but I imagine it to be so. It was stupid of me not to ask your father about their relationship but hey, love is a complex disease. Lizzie, stop touching the potty! It's still wet. Don't worry, I will show you the painting once it is done. I already made a sketch and then I will fill it in with color. I will make it so astounding that your father will yearn and swoon for her. And that's better than mummification."

I do not know if I can move on after what Miss Paardekoper told me. I pedal towards home and Father will ask me why I am late. I will tell him that my rear tire was deflated. He must not know that I had been at Miss Paardekoper's.

Father is busy in his garden when I arrive. He is intent on seeding his vegetables. He has read in an encyclopedia that you can sow cabbage, savoy cabbage, zucchini and celery in June. He is on his knees as he digs on the ground. He does not notice that I came home late. I go straight to the shed and pump up my tire.

"Hello, Lizzie," he welcomes me. "How was school? Tonight we will have dinner at an Indian restaurant. We are going to celebrate. Mom and I finally split up!"

We take the train to Utrecht. The Indian restaurant is in a basement beside the canal. The place is jam packed with students and people in their thirties. I am embarrassed that I am the only child in the crowd.

"I will order a variety of snacks and dishes so you will get a taste of real Indian food," Father declares.

I think it's ridiculous. He knows that I have been to India with Miss Paardekoper. We even had dinner in one of the most expensive hotel.

"What do you like to drink, Lizzie? I think you should get a Cola," he suggests.

I choose a tonic. I find it so weird that Dad is like a zombie when Mom is away, but when they split up he turns into a cheerful man. He is suddenly attentive to me. What is he up to?

"Listen, Lies. I'll call you Lies from now on. You can let go of your childish name. You'll see some changes in the next two months. Mom and I are getting divorced. I get to keep the house. I love that house. Your mother will stay in China. She met some gook while she was there and they have their own plans. I do not want her anymore and she does not want me either so it's over. It's wasn't even a relationship to begin with. Anyway, I need to go to India to take care of something… It might take me weeks or months, but I need to do this. I want to move on with my life. I have talked to Miss Paardekoper and you can stay with her for the meantime. She is excited to be with you."

20

I asked Paul to take me to Father although he will only talk
with me. Maybe I can now end my therapy. I will see if I can
leave the sculpture of father in the home of sick people or take
it back to my studio. I still have to decide where to put it.

Father sits on the backseat between Paul and me. I realize
that I love his hands. Is it because I want to hold on to them or
it just my nerves?

Paul decides to keep himself in the background.

"You have to do this on your own," he urges. "I know that
you can do it. I'm so proud of you."

If I leave the past behind, I can go to India with Farhad.

"I need to show you something," he revealed. "Your
journey to India is my gift. I want you to meet my parents and
my family. And I also want to show you the orphanage."

I think it's a good idea. I consider Farhad as my best friend,
and I think that I will never marry him. He's a good man,
although I never asked him if he was gay. He does not mention
anything about women or friends and he does not feel any
passion for me. I love him and it will only get worse if he does
not love me back. I have tried to entice him with my beauty,
but I do not want to seduce him with my body. I want him to
be moved by my inner aesthetic.

He told me that he did not expect me to visit. He did not
realize that I was hitting on him. I was shocked when he
remarked that he was not seduced at all. He likes to come to

me, talk with me and hug me. But there is no spark, no flame. There is only friendship.

Maybe there will come a time when he will desire far more than friendship and I will be more than willing to make a living doll that will bind us forever.

The hall is the nursing home is all too familiar; it was not so long ago when I took Father to this place. I feel the same sickening pain in my stomach once again.

I consulted with Doctor Beunk. "You have to take a look at Dad," I told him. I can't take it anymore. When he came from India, everything took a downturn. He gradually slipped from his routine, he no longer worked in the garden. We used to eat cabbage and savoy cabbage from his garden but then we reverted back to pizza. He drowned in cynicism, he was once again cold and cruel. I do not know what happened in India, he does not want to talk about it but I think he was hurt and disappointed from his failed journey. When Father left, he was a spirited and hopeful man. He decided to move on after the divorce. But that man never returned. His hand trembled and sometimes he chased me with a knife. It happened when I was about to finish my studies in the Academy. He left the gas stove on while he sat in his pajamas on the street. He had no idea what time or day it was. I do not know if he played a fool to escape reality or he was getting mad. He was unstable and unpredictable. I did not feel safe with him anymore. When I confronted him about the incident, he looked at me lovingly and told me I was joking. "Me? A knife? Lizzie, you are such a prankster. He thought that it was just a silly game.

Doctor Beunk asked me to bring him to his clinic, but Father refused. Eventually the doctor came for a house call.

Father was very alert, he acted properly as if he knew that something important was about to happen.

"I'm sorry, doctor. My daughter wants me gone." He remarked.

I had never talked to him about my plans and yet he said in a credible way. He understood that it was a last ditch effort.

"Is that so, Lalitha?" Doctor Beunk inquired.

I lowered my eyes to the ground.

"Ask him how many one and one is," I suggested to the physician. I did not want to meet Father's gaze

"Two," Father said instantly. "I am not crazy!"

The doctor was about to leave when Father said: "Sir, she wants to drink but her school doesn't allow it," he continued.

Beunk was satisfied with his observation.

"What do you do all day, Mister Backs, if I may ask?"

Father fiddled with his hands. It was not Parkinson's but it was from fear. Fear of the inevitable.

"I help my daughter to school as soon as my wife leaves for work. Then I go to the office."

"Does your wife still live here?" the doctor added.

"What do you mean?" Father asked.

"I've heard that she's been in China for eight years."

He shuffled in his chair and he glared at me. I coughed to mask my pain.

"How about you, Mr. Backs. What do you do again?"

He did not answer.

Stop it, doctor. I said to myself. He's been tortured enough. I feel like a sadistic Japanese guard. He needs to go, there is no other way. He is untenable and I have suffered long enough.

"Mr. Backs, it seems that you're a little sick. You might want to loosen your jacket so I can listen to your breathing."

Father starts unbuttoning the first five buttons, loosens his coat and then closes it gain. His hands fumble at the doctor's instructions.

"That bitch wants me gone, Doctor. She wants to live with a bad guy instead of her own father. You bastard!"

His words sting my ears and pierce my soul. I hold on to the wheelchair, hands trembling. Paul told me to replace the "B word" with 'basta' or 'backsta' but I cannot get over it. The connotation remains stabbed in my heart.

"Are you okay?" Paul asks me.

"I think I need to sit down for a while." I reply.

A few months after Dr. Beunk's visit, Father and I along with Miss Paardekoper walk down the hall towards his clinic.

"You're not going to drop me off, huh? I've been to a Japanese prison camp and I do not want to go to hell again."

He lays his head on my shoulders.

"Don't do this to me, Lizzie. The POW camp is enough. I do not want to stay here."

I never understood why someone so demented such as him could clearly understand what was going on. They say that pigs respond differently when they are transported to the slaughterhouse. They think that it is unfair.

The nurses are nice to him.

"Bert, it will only be a while. It's just for observation." Eva Paardekoper addressed my father with his first name. Bert Backs, that's my father's full name.

"We'll pick you up soon."

I am not sure if he understands that it is an empty promise. There is no soon. He will stay here and wait for his death.

A nurse talks to us in the hallway outside the office. "You can come back tomorrow and you'll see that you've made the right decision. We'll take good care of him."

I did not go back.

I push father down the hall. No one notices him, they are accustomed to seeing him.

We get into the elevator and go up to the first floor. I feel my arms are sweaty. How long has it been since I last visited? A month? I do not know. We open the door that leads to the living room. Professor von Habert welcomes us at the door. "Oh, how nice of my former students to visit. Can I help you with something?"

We walk down the hall and enter the living room. I push the cart forward. Someone approaches father, shakes his hand and runs into the same mannerism characteristic of Parkinson's. Is there oxygen here? I wonder because it smells like the windows are rarely opened.

I see Father standing in front of a window. I am appalled. He has grown thinner and he stares into space. He looks like the doll in my cart. If they sit beside each other, no one can tell the difference. I look around and see that Paul is talking to someone at the end of the hallway. Is that a nurse or a resident? I cannot tell. I carefully push my cart past five people sitting near Father.

"Good day," I greet them as I pass by. Some say bye, others nod while some look up and then stare at their hands as if something was wrong with their clothes. I slide the wheelchair next to Father and sit down.

"Hello, Father." I say.

"Who is that man?" Father turns to Paul, who is standing next to me. I feel happy and disappointed at the same time.

I visited him a few days ago and he did not recognize me. I guess he did not even miss me. The past is solid and then thawed and washed away. It drains in the sewer of civilization that not even Mother can dig out.

"How are you?" I ask him.

He silently slid his chair and walks away. It seems that they all wear crepe soles. I see his diaper bulge from the back of his pants. His hair is neatly combed and he is wearing the vest that he had on when Dr. Beunk visited him.

"Let him go," Paul suggests. "He'll come right back. It's strange that people with dementia wander around. No one knows why."

A lady of seventy sits across me and I watch her as she wriggles a tablecloth. Her hands pause for a moment. She smiled at me and she pushes her lower teeth forward. I suppose that those are dentures, I am familiar with the elderly having dental implants. I look at her dry, coarse hands. I assume that she comes from a farming family. Her hands show years of hard labor on the land. It was the type of hands that never had the time for a book. She stays up late in the evening to finish her chores and wakes up early the next morning to tend for her flocks and children.

My imagination runs wild, I love drama. Who knows, she might even be a spinster. Here in the nursing home, the rich and the meager live under one roof. It is a house of gloom.

Paul informs me that people who had severe dementia were housed in the upper floor. His aunt was in that section and Paul visited her once. When he approached, a rattled man stood by the door. "Open the door!" Paul cried. Paul and a nursing aide rushed inside and saw that her aunt was sitting in a corner. She immediately recognized him. A man stood beside her and he insisted that she was his wife and to prove his point he dropped his pants and started to drive to her. Her aunt did not respond. The nurse told them that she was disoriented, but it wore off in a few days. She was back to normal. Her aunt was eventually allowed to join the ward for people with tolerable dementia. She lived there for four years until she succumbed to pneumonia.

Father comes back and walks straight at me.
"Day Lies," he was surprised. "What are you doing here?"
I stand up and give him a hug.
"You do not have to cry," he consoles me.
He sits down in front of the cart and looks at his replica.
"Is that your father?" he asks with a sweet voice.
"Yes." I reply.
"What is it?"
He shrugs. I start with India. I've read that it is best to begin with the most recent past, the day when he said nothing.
"Beautiful women in India." He tells me.
He beams. I get a picture from my bag. It is a photo of the painting of the Indian woman that Eve Paardekoper made. He strokes the paper and smiles.
"You can keep it. I will the picture later in your room, next to your cabinet."
He looks at me sweetly for a long time.
"You are too beautiful," he remarked.
"Do not cry, Ma'am," he tells me after a moment.
He picks up a napkin and hands it to me.
"Do I know you from somewhere?"
"I'm your daughter, Lizzie."
He smiles.
"You're still a child in a Japanese prison camp, eh Father?"
I try.

He nods hesitantly.

"Not funny," he adds.

He shakes his head, get up and walks out of the room.

I take the trolley with father's replica and go into the hallway. Father walks in circles. He comes back at me for the second time and he looks puzzled at the man in the cart.

"Hey, Lizzie." He calls out.

He gives the doll a shove and he runs as if nothing happened. His head bounces happily. I guess I can get rid of the doll already.

Mom does not even know that he is in a nursing home. She has not heard anything from father in years. She occasionally sends a Christmas card but she has not written me since I was at the Academy. I don't mind. If ever I have children, I will never let them down.

I walk to his bedroom and see that there are three beds. They all look the same and I have no idea which is his. The tables next to the beds are lined with pictures of family members. I see a picture of me. Now I remember that I had left him a photo album. I get the picture of the Indian woman and insert it in the leather bound frame and put it in his locker next to my picture. I do not see Mom's picture, I guess I forgot to put one in. I open his drawer out of curiosity. There is a pen, more photos and dentures. Father does not have any dentures. Someone must be missing a few teeth.

Underneath a notebook is a statue that is vaguely familiar. It is a figurine of a nude female with big, round breasts in a sitting position with a shawl on her shoulders. The waist is very narrow and the head looks like a mask and two thick braids stand upright. The bronze statue is about ten inches high. I have no idea how he took it. I think it was a statue from mom's trip to India.

I hide the statue in the doll's jacket. No one will know it is there. Father will not miss it. I feel guilty, but I consider it my duty to keep the heirloom safe. It has to remain in the family and if I leave it here, it might fall into the wrong hands.

"There you are," Paul spots me.

I fear that he has seen me take the statue.

"Can we go? I have another appointment and it's quite a long ride."

We say goodbye to father. This is better for all of us.

I push the cart into the parking light. I take father out of the wheelchair and put him on the backseat. I lift the cart and put it in the compartment and sit on the passenger seat beside Paul. We sit in comfortable silence.

"How do you feel now?" He asks me once we are out of Schiedam.

"I do not know... empty... sad... Ideally, I want to take him with me. I hope he dies soon. I could give him an injection or a Drion pill and I will be doing him service. He has no one and he cannot even recognize his own daughter. He does not hate me, his unwanted child. He has nothing."

We stop at New York Hotel to grab a snack. Paul needs to go meet his appointment. I take father from the backseat and place him on the window seat in the corner of the restaurant. I frequent the newly-opened place because of the pleasant atmosphere and good food. When I sit down, I realize that I am right across the street where Farhad lives. It did not occur to me that I was in Rotterdam. I never considered the place with an international character when it is the usual meeting place for writers and artists.

"You've done very well, Lalitha. I'm impressed. Do you feel that the hate is gone and you have shaken your father loose?"

He ordered the baked salmon skin while I take the sole.

"Care for some white wine?"

We check in. The tower room is still available.

Farhad is on the other side of the Meuse. He is my unattainable love while I share my bed with Paul, my therapist.

21

How long have I made father's wax image? I narrowed it down and transferred him from an Ikea to a soft, bright red armchair. He sits like a king. I change his clothes. He now wears a colorful shirt that the men in India wear, and there is a tuft of dark chest hair underneath. I used Farhad's chest hair. "I shall shave twice a year," he promised. Given his father's age it should be gray but I decided it was better in black. I pulled up the corners of his mouth. I want him to look haughty and optimistic. I want hope shine in his eyes, unlike the painting in my studio.

Father will go to India with me. He travels in a large suitcase. India is his final resting place, the land of his beloved, though his love was unrequited. I'll find out why.

I keep the Indian statue in my hand. I have never seen such a remarkable female form in real life. Father must have bought it or found the piece when he was in India for a few months with Mom. Have they unearthed it together? I never heard of it but it might explain what went wrong between them. I think that he did not buy it, it could well be a four thousand year old artifact from the Mohenjodaro. The complex was exposed after an earthquake. Mohenjodaro was an impressive city with 35,000 inhabitants complete with sewage and numerous water sources and shops. It was a trading center where art was sold to Sumer and Mesopotamia. It was an advanced civilization that was more or less wiped out with the flood. What remained after the flood were the bronze statues of elegant, naked dancers with arms full of bracelets like the one father had. Jan Piersson, the Director of the Art School at that time came with his friend and Curator of the Museum of Ethnology appraised the artifact and told me that it was a very precious find. The Curator immediately offered me 6,000 Guilders for the statue. "It is very rare," he said. "no other museum in the world has it. Be careful, Lalitha."

I held on to the bronze statue.

Father is getting more mysterious. I wish he could talk about his experience in India then perhaps we can become friends. There are so many unanswered questions and I hope that Mom has the answers. I do not even know if she is alive. She is unaware that Father is in a nursing home. She spits on Chinese soil while Father drifts further and further to a shadowy world.

22

My sculpture grows. I cannot edit the form, neither determine its color. It is molded with invisible hands, kneaded in my history; it inherits my scars and my dreams. I have to wait until it becomes visible. It has its own identity after years and decades have passed. Its personality bears traces of my own, the causal agent in all of us.

Whose tracks do I carry? I cannot say anything about my child's father. My mother could not even shield me from the greatest of all suffering. I was a caveman.

"Will you keep it?"

He asked me sweetly, but it felt like murder. I have destroyed two images because I heard Father's disapproving tone in my head. I could see the contempt in his eyes as he told me countless times that I was too stupid and worthless. I was already an adult when I broke them. I buried the shards as if they were my children. The images are alive; they exist with a purpose; whether it is love, anger or hatred. They are never meaningless.

What do I know about my natural mother? Was she happy when she felt my hands for the first time? Did she caress my skin with her finger? Did she cradle me in her arms or did she despise me? As if I was made of rubbish. Is an unwanted child enough reason to be sad? Shouldn't all babies be welcomed with happiness?

Now that I'm more mature and pregnant, I long for my mother and my father who never wanted me. I do not understand how that could be possible. A man needs to belong somewhere. He needs to have an origin. Does it make any difference?

"Will you keep it?"

He was referring to the baby but his words reminded me of my broken creations and it felt like hailstones in my ear.

I immediately enclosed my belly with my arms to protect it, in the hope that the question would never reach my child. I did not yet know its gender, but I was certain that she is a girl.

"Of course I want to keep her, Farhad."

I said it in a whisper that he did not hear it.

He patted me on the head and pulled me close. We hugged for a few minutes.

"Sensible," he said. "Very good. But I think it's better if we postpone our trip to India."

"No, we have to go. I need to know who my real parents are." I insisted.

"And Paul? Is Paul coming too?"

Paul was immediately enchanted with me. I was his first love. He was ashamed that he had sex with a client that night in the New York Hotel. I never noticed him as more than my therapist. He was not aloof, and he was not intrusive. He was always around when I needed him, but he never showed any affection towards me. He was correct, courteous and charming, but I never noticed his good attributes because I was so busy with myself and dad that I never realized that he was a man. He was my mentor, advisor, helper and supporter, but I did not feel a spark between us. Paul was like a drug, you swallow it without even thinking. You feel better and get well but you do not realize that the drug has transformed you. It was Farhad I wanted. I talked about love, life and my future with Paul but I never asked for his views until the day we visited Father together in the nursing home. That served as my resignation as a client, or whatever it could be called. I was free, and he was free, though not quite. For the first time I noticed his feigned interest in me, not as a psychologist, but as a human being.

Paul told me that the therapist was gone.

He tells me that I am his first love. The expert therapist suddenly becomes shy, insecure and even vulnerable. His uncertainty gave me strength.

"In retrospect, I realize that I studied psychology so I could understand myself better. Everyone thought that I was confident boy who mastered the game and knew all the codes. But deep down I was a hesitant child. I've accepted that fact and I am trying to deal with it."

My therapist exposed himself, showed his vulnerability and because of that, I noticed him.

The overnight stay at the hotel was my idea, I did not want to lose him.

Paul is going to India with me. He wants to know everything about me- my background, even my parents. "Our child has the right to know." He declares as he caresses my belly. He plays with my navel that is sticking up from the bulge.

I can still fly; I'm only fourteen weeks pregnant. My waist is slightly thicker. Paul gently touches my breasts, they are sensitive and I can hardly imagine that I am the first woman he has ever made love with. He is concerned and would do anything for me.

We will move in together after our trip to India. We have to look for a suitable property for our life together. His dreary town house won't do and my apartment is too small.

"We will call her Eva. Is that okay? Eva is a lovely name."

After a few days, we are certain that the baby is a girl. He knows Miss Paardekoper from my stories, but does not know that her name is Eva. I feel like it is a tribute to the woman who gave me my life. Eva.

"As of now we do not talk about the baby, but Eva." Paul tells me as he showers my naked body with tender loving kisses. He puts his head to my belly and turns his head just above my belly button.

"Do you hear that Eva? If Mom is going to marry me then your name will be Eva Adama."

We make love, we move with tenderness rather than passion.

His body is not particularly muscular, he is rather slim and a bit stiff. He has blond hair with a plain face. Maybe that it is why I never noticed him. He was not attractive. I saw him as a guy that I could talk to, who listened to me and who gave me good advice. I never saw him as a potential partner. Now I see him and I admire his calmness and his ability to keep things in perspective. I feel safe with him, not with his body but with his balance, his insight. He makes me feel important, loved and attractive.

"Is that a marriage proposal? I did not realize that your name and mine sounds predestined. Eva Adama!

Lalitha and Eva Adama."

It's crazy, but after the sweet lovemaking in the hotel, we never spoke to each other. I thought about him every day, but I never called. Paul thought about me, but he was too shy to call me. When I discovered that I was pregnant and the test confirmed it, I called Paul. I had an exceptional alibi. I had no idea how he would react. I barely know him. Would such a man refuse my calls?

"I have something important to discuss with you," I began.

"Is it about your father? Did something wrong happen to him?"

"About a sculpture, I want to talk to you about a particular image. It is still a concept and I want to discuss it with you. Can you come over?"

I often talked about my paintings and he has seen a couple of my paintings in my studio at The Hague.

He had no idea and he was totally surprised. I did think that he could prepare himself with the news and I wanted to see how he would spontaneously react. That would certainly tell me something about my future husband. I see him enter the room. He was on his bike and he had a blush on his cheeks. The wind was still in his air. He threw his long raincoat on the bench.

I set him in front of a painting of a father and a girl. It was Dad and me on the same canvas. I was a happy, carefree girl without fear. The painting marked my freedom. I finally let go of the past. Dad was out of my system and nothing could hold me back. I loved the girl on the canvas. She was vulnerable but hopeful.

He looked at the painting for some time and then I watched as it hit him. He was out of control for a moment. He restrained a smile. Were his eyes moist?

"Are you that girl?"

"What makes you think that?"

"The eyes. An open look. I'm a dreamer, a sweet dreamer. A child in harmony."

I immediately felt good. He was certainly the father of my child.

"Paul, I'm pregnant."

He looked at me incredulously.

"Since when?"

"Since the New York Hotel."

He held me in his arms, he kissed me deeply.

The questions about how and what to do with the child came later. We focused on the two of us.

We decided to see each other more often so we could get to know each other better. He only knew one side of me and I only saw an aspect of his personality. His idea to create a painting of Father was brilliant. It was a new and original idea. Because of him I was able to understand the images that dictated my life. I painted myself as a child and I lived in my pictures, but I had no picture of him.

Farhad is looking for a suitable property that we can live in, preferably with a studio or a property near my apartment so I could keep my studio.

I was afraid of Farhad's reaction but he thinks Paul is a great guy. A very fitting man for me. He announced that he would accompany us to India.

PART 2

MAMA

23

I ask if he can take us further. The Land Rover is constantly spewing out black smoke. I can smell it, it stinks. Eva is so fragile. How long is she now? Eighteen inches, something like that. She has fingers and she can smell, taste and touch. She deserves fresh, clean air.

He assures me that they have a spare truck just in case something bad happens. If you travel with just one and have bad luck, you might freeze to death.

I think we are almost fifty feet up the mountains and it is a sufficient height.

It is almost white around us. We drive as long as possible. We walk for the rest of the journey, Paul, me and Eva. Father's upper torso dangles from my backpack. It's the only way that he could fit and I could carry him.

Farhad knew a specialist in New Delhi who sold stuff for tours in the Himalayas. Now we are clothed in thermal underwear and clothes that will keep us warm. We have Eskimo boots on our feet and everything else that we could possibly need for the trip.

The drivers know the way. We made the ascent with ease. We had a stopover at 3,000 feet and now we are at 4,000 feet above sea level. It is not the best time of the year to go up the mountain, but I could not postpone the trip. Eva is growing, and if a bit further with the pregnancy it will too exhausting for me and it will dangerous for her. Eva can stay at home after I give birth, but I will surely miss her. And so, now is the most appropriate time.

Father deserves a grave in the perpetual snow. Then I can finally put him to rest and I will finally end the bitter chapter in my life.

I now understand him better. If only he told me everything.

Paul looks worried, he understands that I need to say goodbye, but he is concerned about Eva.

A pregnant woman cannot stay long at such a high altitude especially if you're not used to it. He thinks that I can pass father to the real climbers, but I refuse to let go of him. Not just yet.

We left Delhi early in the morning. I had to pee a lot at night and I had to drink plenty of water. You have to drink gallons of water every day, otherwise you will get massive headaches and breathlessness. You can also try swallowing painkillers, but I would rather endure a headache rather than harm Eva.

It does not take long before we find a nice spot. We did a hole and lay father on his eternal grave of virgin snow.

But first we have an overnight stay. We cannot walk too fast; our bodies need to adjust to the cold environment.

We slept in a hut yesterday. We saw pilgrims dressed in leather aprons and leather sleeves. After a long walk, they fold their hands to their face. Then they take out a kind of slippers from the pocket of their aprons, kneel down and stretch on the snow for as long as possible, the slippers in their hands and their foreheads on the ground. They continuously repeat the gesture as they make their way up the mountain. I am awed at their devotion. How far do they go? Some go to the caves where important saints, such as Guru Rinpoche, the teacher of the fourteenth Dalai Lama went to meditate. He has spent more than ten years in silent seclusion to ponder about love and compassion. Jesus only spent forty days in the wilderness while he spent thirteen years in seclusion. He chose to live in solitude fifteen years after his master died. He lived in caves and became a hermit. His whereabouts are an inspiration for monks and for all those who hope to understand who and why we are. The pilgrims hope to obtain an inner compass that will guide them as an infallible captain brings others to a land of liberation. They want to find an inner guru who would guide them like the sun and the moon through the darkness of ignorance and attain overflowing compassion.

As we drive in the desolate beauty of the Himalayas, I now realize that Mohammed had started his vocation in isolation much like the Dalai Lama.

The real pilgrims travel on foot. A horse in an exception. Some move through the mountains for a year. I spoke to a man who encircled the sacred mountain thirteen times as he stretched his body and walked on where his forehead ended. He stretched once again, and he repeated the same ritual until he had reached the height of 5,400 meters with the bitter cold and lashing winds beating on his body.

How does an enlightened human being feel? Self respect? Is it security at having achieved the unimaginable?

It seems to me that self control was the ultimate goal for many Buddhists. Isn't the lonely self sacrifice a waste of energy? Or does seclusion guarantee a break from the past and the present and a clear road to the future? I understand the need for contemplation and it can be very inspiring but perhaps others are merely escaping the unsolvable. Is it the

Ben Bouter

inability of others to avoid hurt and desire the reasons that drove Mom to this forlorn journey?

I notice that the Land Rover has stopped. We drive until we reach the other car. There is no one else around besides Paul, me and the two drivers. It starts to snow. Our driver gets out to see what is going on. We are well prepared for the trip and we have plenty of water with us.

The car is stuck in a hole and the wheel is bent. The jeep cannot take us any further. They decide to go to the next hut with a car then they can call for help and pick us up the next morning.

We see herds of colossal yaks together with their shepherds and dogs that keep them intact. The heavy beasts and the Nomads are in constant motion although it is often fifty degrees below zero. They have everything at hand- tents, blankets, hand mills, a brazier, looms and even carpets. The yaks carry the heavy load of bowls, holy books and mantras on their backs. The yaks are at the head of the pack as they search for water and grass. The goats, sheep and horses follow them to their next destination. The yaks are their lifeblood. Their tents are made from durable materials that last for generations. Milk and butter are their elixirs.

The shepherds go down while we go up. The trek is dangerous.

They sell sheep wool and pashiminas and mountain goats. The wool is more expensive then cashmere. It is rare and of a softer and finer quality. Around May the animals are sheared and the wool is sold. They cannot remain up in the mountains for so long because of the heavy snowfall. Buddhists and

Muslims have been doing business with each other for decades and they mutually respect each other.

There is less and less visibility. The wiper pushes off the snow from the glass with difficulty. I see a gray shape in the distance that resembles a large house. Is this our home for the night?

Paul is strangely quiet. The cars are old and we had to stop a few times because the fuel filter was contaminated. He does not want any of these inconveniences. I have to complete the journey and go back to New Delhi otherwise, I cannot say goodbye to Father.

I feel my stomach. What do you think, Eva? Do you like it here? This is India, the land where Mommy was born!

It's not a house, it's a monastery. I should have realized that there were no houses in this area. It is two kilometers away. I can feel the tension in the air as the driver struggles to bring us to our destination. Too bad I cannot watch the snow. I have to make it on top of the mountain, which is the only place where I can pay my respects.

The jeeps stops, and the driver steps out.

"Here it is," Jag announces.

Jag is the younger driver and the funnier of the two. His name means "universe." When we met, he said to me with a mischievous smile: "Lalitha, Jag." Our names meant "most of the universe" when combined. He pointed at me and gave Paul a thumbs-up.

He talks a lot. He relates how he learned to read and write in the monastery when he was six years old as did most of the boys in his village. Each day started with prayers at half past five then they had salty tea and roasted barley flour with butter for breakfast. They rolled the dough into a ball and threw it in the air as a gesture to the gods and after which they ate it. The Sherpas and the nomads eat it, it is easy to prepare and easy to digest. Sometimes they even add oats, rice or wheat to the flour.

I have never visited a Tibetan monastery when I was a child.

The lessons begin after breakfast. They are taught music, rituals and sacred dances during the first six years.

"Then you choose between the philosophical college or the artistic and liturgical movement as your vocation. But I left the monastery when I was fifteen." Jag relates.

He lives in the village. But when the winter makes it impossible for him to work and the village is isolated due to the weather, he keeps himself busy with contemplation.

He has a wife and a child.

"Two children, actually. But the girl did not make it, she was stillborn. One in every two children die during or after birth," he says with a smile of acceptance. Such is the life of many nomads, no doctors, no surgery or medicine to stop the bleeding. The only thing we rely on is the experience of older women. Going to a hospital is impossible at this time of the year."

I rub my belly. We will be long gone when I deliver Eva. Hey, Eva? You're just sixteen weeks old. Eva means "living" but still, his remarks alarms me. If something really bad happens, then it could be catastrophic.

"My brother is still here in the monastery." Jag continues. "He has studied for nine years at the college and he is now teaching philosophy and art classes. I'll introduce you to him."

They carry our stuff upstairs, sixty or seventy packs to be sure. The monastery is open for everyone. Typical Tibetan flags flutter everywhere. Young and old monks walk together. Jag shows us the way. He walks across the courtyard to the stairs. He leaves our backpacks on the bottom step and he climbs up the stairs. Moments later, he comes down the steps with a bald monk in a typical brown-red rode. He is barefoot. It seems quite incomprehensible at this altitude.

He has the same eyes as Jag, but looks older. His skin is hardly modified by the inclement weather and he has a smooth clear face compared to Jag who looks dingy. Jag's older brother speaks immaculate English.

Paul is now talking to another monk who apparently speaks German, He points to the yellow cloth with red bands that are filled with brightly-colored ribbons. In one corner of the monastery is a painted wooden Buddha. I walk towards it and examine the figure up close. Painstaking work, I immediately think and it is done with great precision. I see a black Buddha in a sitting position. He has a green leaf behind his head and he is poised in some sort of sun with gossamer, wavy wire like the heart of a flower; a naked white woman embraces him. Her legs are partially folded on his back as his hands support her buttocks. It seems that they are making love. There are clouds around them and something reminiscent of a green meadow. It was probably painted a long time ago.

"This is the most excellent primordial Buddha," Jag's brother tells me as he is now diagonally behind me. "Typical of Tibetan Buddhism. Do you know that Buddhism varies from one country to another? Our tradition is quite different from that of China and Thailand."

I had no idea.

"Our mantra plays a bigger role. Do you know what mantra is?"

He asks in a very friendly tone, eager to teach.

He carries my backpack and runs smoothly up the stairs. Paul carries his. Dad dangles up and down in a certain cadence while Jag's brother walks up the steps. He brings us to our room where we will spend the night. We go back down the stairs and say farewell to Jag and the other driver.

The monk asks us if we want some bread. I accept his offer, but Paul requests if the butter could be lessened. Jag's brother laughs.

"You too?" he asks me.

I fold my palms together and make a slight bow to endorse the request.

"Do you know what mantra means?"

"Just weird syllables that you endlessly repeat," Paul answers as he bites into his bread.

That's a sign that he's at ease. His humor has returned.

"I walk back to the image of the black Buddha and the intense white woman. What is this painting doing with all these religious men around?" I do not notice that Jag's brother is beside me.

"You paint," he tells me.

I am speechless.

"How did you know?"

"You look like a painter. Come with me."

He takes us to a room that looks like a studio.

"Painting can be done in different ways," he began. "You can paint anything as realistic as possible. It is a useful exercise as you look, mix colors and perfect your technique. You can also paint your own interpretation of reality, what you feel, think about it. You can also use the traditional Buddhist approach. That's what we do here. Everything is according to the prescribed patterns, colors and proportions so that gods can recognize each object. The brow of one god entails days of concentrated work.

Our brushes, paint and compasses are tools from our gods and you should respect these utilities.

We say the mantra of the god while we are painting. Painting is a form of sacred service."

I see their artworks are beautiful and made with devotion, but religious art is not for me. I do not like paintings that have a sacred value. They detach objects from the earth and give it an ethereal force. I do not follow their thinking. Their devotion to the supernatural images are acceptable but they should recognize the more earthier forms, like the farmers who work on their fields and they take part of the bounty. But I will not argue. Respect belongs to this region. Muslims and Buddhists live together peaceably.

The snow continues to fall. The monks retired to their beds early, and we do the same. I am here in a Buddhist monastery and I lie next to Paul, my former therapist and one great love. I feel happy. We have converged without realizing it. It is not love, but understanding, listening and kinship that have alloyed us together. We lie down next to each other and stare at the colorful wooden ceiling above us. The crown of the Himalayas is covered in snow.

It happened near here. Why? He had hope in his eyes when he left. But something happened to him when he was in India and he changed after that. He no longer saw the future, not even the moon. I am sorry that it has slain him and I can no longer tell him the logic and the facts that I have discovered. His life was stripped from his body in this mountain range. How many dreams have died here? His mental capacities have escaped him and he hangs lifeless in a chair, restless in bed next to others who have lost their minds and weep for an unexpected gift. I will not that happen.

"Would you please read an excerpt from the diary? Maybe that can help me sleep. We have a big day ahead of us. Wait..."

I take dad out of my backpack and put him next to us on the spacious bed.

"Listen, dad. Listen..."

I change my mind. I ask Paul not to read it. We need to wait. We need to sleep.

24

When we wake up, the monks have long been busy with their activities. We make our own breakfast. I find it striking that the kids enjoy their time here. They looked very happy and relaxed.

I feel my stomach. Soon, Eva will have her own fingerprint. She is unique and no one will have the same imprint as she has. She is Eva.I hear the words of Miss Paardekoper. She's right.

Eva is a brand new image. Will she have blond hair? My eyes? Blond hair and dark eyes will be wonderful. Everything is beautiful as long as she is healthy and happy. I can feel her in just a few more weeks.

Paul puts his ear to my belly as he expresses his daily mantra: "we love evaevaevaevaevaevaeva youuuuuuuuuuuu," followed by kisses around my belly button. He even adapted the melody to the sounds of the monastery.

I hope that Father will see Eva when she is born and he can touch her when we are home again. I will feel equally happy in any case.

It snowed all night. It fell so quietly that I never heard it fall. We look out the vast plain above us all the way to the vast mountain range. Jag's brother gives us sticks to help us walk easier.

"Always keep to the narrow path on the left, stay on the side of the mountain and if it starts to snow, use the stick like a blind man does. Come back right away and make sure that you feel the ground under your feet and beside you. Repeat it like a mantra. It will keep you safe. If it snows hard, you will see nothing and the path will be treacherous. If you have gone too far to come back, you can look for a long pole with flags on the left. Exactly a hundred paces further on the same left is a deep cave where you can hide. The mouth of the cave can be reached with a rope ladder. One of our monks may still reside in the cave. He has been there for three years. Don't mind him. The cave is safe. There are blankets there. Take a lighter and some matches. You can continue with your journey once the snow stops. If you take too long, I will come to you. Have a good trip."

He makes a bow with his palms at the height of his heart.

We both have our backpacks, but not all our stuff. Father's head dangles from Paul's backpack and it makes a pretty sight. I have made the corners of his mouth merrier and he looks like a curious child. He is not cold in any case.

The path is narrow and difficult. There is a ravine right next to us and it makes a breathtaking sight. We ease our way to through. The height impedes us from walking faster and I do not want to take any risks.

The sticks are a good idea and fortunately there are enough sticks to last the entire trek. I try to remember the path in my head, but the snow makes recall difficult. The landscape constantly changes and every curve makes a spectacular show. The snow under my feet is bearable and it looks like we're the first people on a newly discovered planet. I am blissfully happy. Has anyone made it this far?

I stop after fifteen minutes. The trek is more difficult than I expected. Sometimes I have trouble breathing. The road is steep and slippery here and there. We see the monastery in the distance with the many waving flags and we see dots that resemble humans, herds of yak and sheep. My eyes are the only visible part of my face and the rest is covered: a wool hat, a scarf around my face and thick mittens. We also have binoculars.

It is pleasantly cold and the stunning view repels the freezing cold. The biting wind makes it colder that no thermometer can indicate.

We see the prayer flags flutter along the Himalayan road. We can also hear them flap in the wind at night. The wind is our constant companion in our journey. It sculpts the mountains through the centuries and it provides a new scenario. The wind forms interesting shapes, quirky, charming, menacing.

I read that the prayer flags were introduced in Tibet in the eleventh century but were used earlier in the Indian side of the Himalayas. The printed mantras of various Buddhas and sacred texts flutter in the wind as radio messages to the gods: save mankind from suffering, remove all suffering and bring us luck! Air, rain and sun attack the sacred texts, making them part of the universe. Eventually the world will be filled with pure and noble thought that there will be no room for evil.

"We cannot stand too long," Paul says with worry. "We have to keep moving or else we will get rigid and stiff. Cold is dangerous and we still have a long way."

He's right. Our journey has just begun. We cannot sit down because the wind and fatigue will wear us down and we will fall asleep to our deaths. How many have died in this mountain?

The snow sticks to my boots. I try to hit the snow with a stick and check the ground underneath my feet. I have long pants and a woolen skirt like most women to protect me from the cold. Paul has black ski pants and a black ski jacket. The black color absorbs the rays of the sun and it gives a stark contrast in the amazing world of white.

I do not know how far we've gone, but I am certain that we nowhere halfway. I have not seen the stick with flags neither the lips of the cave. Two kilometers is not that far but under these heavy conditions, it can be quite a challenge. I need to rest every now and then and I have pains in my back. My stomach feels heavy. Paul takes pictures whenever we stop. He is impressed with the grandeur. The thick layer of snow enhances the natural beauty of the landscape. I wish Eva could see it. It is so beautiful! Paul embraces me and gives me a greasy kiss on the lips. We laugh. A big kiss! It's wonderful that I met him and we know each other really well.

His parents are still alive. They are a lovely and sweet couple. They are proud of the son. It is nice to know that his family still exists.

I did not know that a psychology student needs to be very good in mathematics and statistics. Research on human behavior often requires a lot of computation. Paul wanted to know how your upbringing affects you and what role does your genes play in determining your behavior. He also wanted to know the various mental disorders and how they can be cured. Paul wanted to do more than just research and his counselor advised him to venture into the therapeutic side of psychology. I am glad that he did, otherwise I would never had known him. I am glad that I do not need to be a psychologist so he could watch me and my reactions. He is at times uncertain with himself and relies on me. I feel like I am his complement and that gives me confidence about the future. Paul and I, together with Eva and maybe, even more children. That would be nice. The air is thinner. The mountain range above us looks bright, but the air is grayer around us. We must be almost halfway, but the stick with the fluttering mantras is still nowhere in sight. I hope it snows once again. Paul tells me that we can no longer walk back to the monastery and I do not want to. I have to make the trip or else the snow will make it difficult for me to go further.

We decide to forgo the drink and eat bread instead. It tastes good. I bite into the brown crust and wash it down with a drink so it goes straight to my stomach. You can get even dehydrated from the wind rather than from the sun. We have to be optimistic and enjoy the breathtaking view.

Jag's brother showed me how to take paintings in the monastery. They are often high and hollow in the inside. The outside is painted by a professional with lots of colors and rare precision. An experienced monk takes a whole day to finish the painting. Once the image is complete, the monks fill it in with mantras made from saffron and water mixed with sacred substances. Then they nail it on the wall. There are thousands of prayers and mantras in one image along with the relics of dead saints: hair, bones, and clothes. They place a heart as the backbone of image while a tree from the mountains symbolizes all kinds of spiritual processes and numerous rites. I always thought that Buddhism was simple without so much superstition, but Tibetan Buddhism is macabre. I do not like the idea that relics are attributed with magical powers. The saints are dead and they do not have any power. I do not want to make any images for them.

It is so impressive that I can walk on fresh snow while there is centuries-old snow underneath. I find it an overwhelming experience, although it is exhausting.

Breathing is almost as difficult. I think that we should not take too long in this altitude because there is so little oxygen. I would hate to think that Eva could get hurt because of the thin air.

The path is now wider and I see some kind of a split. We can continue on the left path, although the paths seem to be straight. I ask for Paul's opinion.

"Jag's brother told us to keep left, and it's best that we heed his advice."

"But he told us to stay on the side of the mountain and he did not mention a fork on the road."

We take a break. I cannot go further unless I get some rest. My back, stomach and chest are aching. Paul also admits that the trek is quite a challenge.

"I'll walk a little further on the left path and check if I see the flags. Then we can rest a little longer inside the cave."

"Please do not stay out too long. We need to stay together."

"I will just take a little walk and I won't go far." He promised.

"Darling, you don't have to look far, every curve is a different picture."

"Just a little. You take a short break. Make sure that you don't go beyond ten minutes." He said as he walked away.

Why Mommy? Why did you have to come here? I do not understand.

Of course I have browsed her diary. It's great that I got it. It's the only keepsake from her except from a handful of pictures. Mom, my mom alone in a cave. For how long and why? She did not indicate that she had a child, who would ignore her own child? I dare not read it in its entirety. Not just yet.

How old was she then? Was she younger than me? I cannot believe that I will soon be able to sit in a place where she spent some time. I felt happy deep down. What went wrong? Why did she give me away? I want to hold her, sit beside her and feel her on my skin. I finally have a mother, a real mother. Farhad told me that she was sweet. Did he tell me that so I won't get offended? He is not much older than me. How did he come know about my birth mother?

Farhad has traveled so far to find me. Was that the reason why he went to The Netherlands? How could he have known? I have so many unanswered questions. How did he know that her aunt was or is my mother? Farhad and I are family! Now I understand why he could not love me. He knew that I had feelings for him but everything turned out fine. Paul is a treasure; he fills me and makes sure that I do not float away to unknown destinations. I will soon transcend reality. Did Mama do just that when she was here for the last few months or weeks of her life? Was the monk there to? Does he know something about my mother?

I get cold even if I am out of the wind. Sitting is not good. I have to keep moving. Too people have froze to death in their reverie.

Where is Paul? I can now see the road up ahead. Perhaps Jag's brother meant that we have to go straight all the way to the left. I struggle to stand up. I feel the wind in my face and I tie the scarf tighter around my head so the wind will not penetrate my face. My eyes are the only visible features on my face. I pause and look at the gray sky. The first snowflakes dance in the wind. Beautiful and dangerous at the same time. We need to find the cave real quick or else we have no choice but to go back. I do not want to die here. I do not want Eva to die. I want to reunite Father to Mama. They need to be together again.

"Paul!"

I hope he can hear me. Maybe it's not a good idea to take the other route and I need to go after him instead. But what's taking him so long? I do not have a watch and I do not know how long he has been out. Has it been ten minutes? I feel that I have suffered a lot longer.

I walk the same path, although the path now looks different. I walk on rocky ground with small steps. A fall will be risky for Eva and I do not want to slip ten meters down a ravine.

I walk a bit further. My vision is blurred; the snow falls harder than before. I am anxious for the first time. I try to encourage myself to keep going. I try to visualize the cave and think of a time when Mom and I sit together in the cave as we read a couple of pages in her diary. She ought to read it, she is entitled to it. Or maybe the diary was written especially for me, so I could learn more about her. Stay focused, I say to myself. You should be brave for Eva. From now on, you need to make your own diary!.

I feel motivated with the thought. Eva is entitled to my diary. She needs to know. She will never see her grandmother. I imagine her reading my diary and her grandmother's diary, maybe when she is also pregnant. It sounds crazy, but that's the time when you find yearn for your origins.

I pull my backpack tighter, so Father is closer to my back as I walk. I hum a song entitled "You'll Never Walk Alone." I have no idea where the song came from. Perhaps the flags blew it in my ear.

25

"Paul!"

I see and hear nothing except the breathtaking mountain range and snow.

I hear my voice echo, but otherwise it's eerily quiet. I continue to walk. I know that cave is much closer than the monastery. Paul did not have to go alone. The snow is coming down at a rapid pace and I is difficult to see. I do not see his footsteps and I do not see anything that indicates that he must have slipped. The snow has covered his tracks. I am now afraid that the snow leopard might come after me. I feel unsafe. Was Mama scared?

No, Lalitha. You cannot think of scary things. Everything will be well. Think of Eva. She continues to live within you and you should be strong for her. Paul is a quiet, sensible man. He is not a daredevil. Something must have happened; otherwise he would have been back by now. You have to be patient. It's all right. You've had enough misery and it's not logical that so many tragedies could befall one family.

Snow is the most beautiful natural phenomenon in these mountains. It is good, everything is good. Keep moving! Remember that people have used this as trade route for centuries to as they make their way to one village from another and to trade and sell things. Why should things go wrong all of a sudden?

I cannot see anymore, it seems that there is a snowstorm. I need to use my stick to make it through each uncertain pass.

You like snow, Lalitha. It has always been your ally. Snow has helped you through childhood. Do you remember that your first sculpture was inspired by snow? Your hands were cold, but that did not hinder you from creating your first masterpiece. Art is your destiny, Miss Paardekoper told you and she told you that your creations would make the world a better place. Everything is possible. Visualize snow as your future dream. You are here on the impressive mountains of the world with your child and your friends. Your future can never be shattered by snow because you have made a pact with your child. The snow is here to protect you, to keep you safe. If you lose your faith, you will lose everything. Do it for Eva, for Paul and do it for Dad because he might not be around to see his granddaughter. Mama died here and it has nothing to do with you. You will later read in her diary that she had a different circumstance. How you respond to adversity is all up to you. Remember wood and gold? They fall in the same fire, but yield different results. You are as valuable as gold. You can do it. People will hang your paintings in the city like they hang mirrors on walls. Do not give up!

Miss Paardekoper is right. I grab my stick and poke on both sides. I slowly inch forward. I shuffle in the deadly silence. I hear the snow change the path under my feet. Nothing is as it seemed.

You'll soon look at this as a beautiful experience. It will be in your memory and it will take form ten years from now. If you think back to this time, Eva will be going to school in the snow. She's nine years old. She is going to run because the snow is to slippery for a bike. Do you see her, Lizzie? She is walking alone. And you can make one of your best images with the seed that is now growing within you.

I shuffle on. I am pleased that Miss Paardekoper is with me. She shows up unexpectedly, and just in time when I really need her. Eva, Eva Paardekoper.

I have so much to live for. Snow will clear up, I assure myself. It will conceal the unimportant things and it will show you the essence of your existence. What this Mom's reason? Mom could have gone to the place for the Saints to contemplate the existence of snow.

I open my palms and feel the snow renew my energy. Step by step I walk towards my goal. I do not need to rush; I just have to keep on going. I prick in front of me, beside me and tap on the ground. I think of all the pilgrims who make their way around the mountain, their bodies stretched on the icy ground as they repeat the ritual over and over. They do not falter. They achieve their goal. Do not whine, Lizzie. Enjoy the challenge. Life without resistance is meaningless. Muscles are generated by the counter pressure.

I prick on the ground, but I do not feel anything. My heart hammers in my chest. I am filled with fear as I realize that I am at the edge of the mountain. I remain still and then slowly turn around so I could go back. I almost lost my balance when I turned. I try to calm myself. I slowly move my left foot slightly backwards. I can feel the ground. Then I drag my right foot to the same distance. I succeed. But I am still in danger. How long can I endure? If I lose my balance, I will certainly fall to my death. I feel like crying. I cannot go on.

I feel something touch my arms and I hear slurred words. This was I was afraid of, delusions.

The cold slowly drives you insane until it solidifies you and stores you in an eternal freezer. Mama must be here somewhere. And father... I remember that father is in Paul's backpack. If I cannot find Paul, then I will never be able to bury father in the snow. I am afraid that I have gone mad. My God, is this my final destination? Is this the fate of our family?

I hear indistinct sounds. Do the Himalayan vultures hover above me? I hear them all day and I think they live in groups. The pressure in my arm increases. Now my arms are in a soft grip in the Himalayas.

"I will ease your suffering," the oracle states in perfect English! I now understood the language. Am I in heaven?

"Come, come with me."

He is pulling gently on my arm, but I refuse his aid. I'm not going with him. I want to find Paul. I do not want to fall into the depths. I want to keep moving forward, and this was negative force that wants to pull me down. Was it mom?

I vaguely see him standing in front of me. There is no ground. It must be a ghost. I think I am going nuts! He is a spirit in the form of a monk.

"Come, Lalitha. Everything is all right. I will take you to Paul."

To Paul... He's definitely dead. The ghosts are coming for me but I will not go with them. There is a baby in my belly. I want to cry... there's a baby in my belly! Eva cannot die, not now!

I cry as I try to fight the madman who is trying to take me away. I have to be careful so I would not lose my balance.

"Go away!" I scream. "You cannot stand on air, You're a ghost from my stupid mind."

He laughs at me and he dances on the floor. He dances as he moves away from me one meter, then two meters. He points at me and he beckons at me to follow him.

I do not know if the vision is real. He has a backpack and he turns towards me with a smile on his face.

"Come on!"

And then I realize that he is Jag's brother.

"Come," he urges me. "Look!"

He jumps and dances again.

"What are you afraid of?"

"You cannot stand. I felt it with my stick. There is no ground!"

He laughs again and he points at my stick. I did not even notice that the snow has stopped falling. I see the path under my feet and I see that I am on solid ground. I look at my stick and realize that my stick is broken; I only hold the upper part in my hands.

Ben Bouter

26

I follow the monk just as he followed me. I did not notice that he walked past me as he ran back to the monastery. He knows the way and he can even run without sight. He heard Paul's cry and he brought him to the cave. He covered him with blankets then he went back to get help. He walked past me like the wind. Then Jag's brother came back with a backpack loaded with medicinal plants and heaven knows what else.

Paul's lower body is paralyzed and he cannot move his legs. He cannot even speak. "Not yet sir, but you can speak tomorrow," Jag's brother told Paul. But he tried anyway. "My wife…" He uttered before he passed out. The monk brought him out of the depths. He could not lie in the snow for so long because he would freeze to death. He might have a broken spine or his neck and he cannot be moved. He's still alive. My Paul, Eva's father is still alive. He lifted him with a rope and brought him inside the cave. He covered him with blankets. He might even pronounce a mantra over him. The monk is now silent as he feels for Paul's pulse.

"Lama is the *amchi* of our monastery," Jag's brother whispers. "He studied at the highest *amchi* school in this area and left the convent school with the highest title. He has studied the eleven main directions of Tibetan medicine as he sat at the feet of the great scholar, the physician of the Dalai Lama."

166

The Lama opens Paul's mouth and he carefully looks at his tongue while his hand continues to hold Paul's wrist. He puts his palm on Paul's forehead. He is serious as he asks Jag's brother to get something from the backpack. He pulls out two bag of powder, sprinkle it in a cup and pour hot water in a bowl. He calmly stirs the potion as he hums. He gives Paul a drink a few moments later. It takes Paul half an hour to finish it. The Lama smiles at me.

I tenderly caress Paul's face. It's my fault that Paul was injured. I kiss him on the forehead and gently kiss his dry mouth. He drifts off to sleep.

I have read Mama's diary. I will tell you what happened:

I will not let them take away my child. It is not the baby's fault. They found out and I know that it should never have happened. But I cannot undo the past. How could I have not known that he was a married man?

I loved the woman from the first sentence that I read in her diary. Mom wanted me to live. Thanks to her, I am here.

I ran away from home today. They wanted to take me to a clinic so they can get rid of my child. How dare they call themselves parents! I hate them! They say that it is for my own good: we are doing it for you darling. This way, you will ensure your future. No man wants to marry a single mother.

Mom, how old were you when you had me? Did the man know that you were pregnant? Did he want me?

The Lama feels Paul's neck. He rubs ointment on him while he hums obscure texts. His head is nestled on a folded

167

blanket. Jag's brother has gone back to the monastery. Father is still in Paul's backpack. I do not have the strength to bury him. Perhaps I should leave him in Mom's cave.

The Lama is now on his stomach next to Paul who now lies on his back. He talks to him in English and I am amazed that the monk can speak a foreign language. The great scholar has the potential to be the future physician of the Dalai Lama. He puts a thin needle on Paul's legs and asks him how he feels. He responds when the needle reaches his pelvis. He can now talk and move his arms.

I read with the light from the burning firewood or actually yak dung. It burns bright. The cave is pleasant and it is larger than I had imagined. There is a pile of holy books in the corner. The Lama is preparing himself for the Dalai Lama. "I will monitor your health," he tells Paul. He studies the writings that the great scholar dictated to him because the books were burned by the Chinese. He knew them all by heart and he wrote the books with his wisdom.

I think of Mom, I see her face before me. She was in the family picture with Mom and Dad when Mom had a research in India. She was the woman that Miss Paardekoper painted-beautiful, soft and fragile. And later on she showed so much strength.

Father was in love all this time and the divorce gave him the freedom to pursue his love. Infatuation made him return to India in the hopes that he could see her again. He probably knew nothing about the pregnancy.

I attend art school. Dad did not approve at first, but he eventually agreed.

I cannot believe it! Art was in our genes. We followed the same route without knowing it. I inherited my passion for sculptures and paintings from her! I try to find out how old she was and her inspiration.

I love Mom and Dad!

I read the phrase nine times. It is written in a large piece of paper, each with a different drawing. They were sketches with minimal strokes, but were creatively made. She had a happy childhood and she had loving parents. I read her diary from the beginning and I realize how happy and carefree she was. But everything changed. Just because their daughter was pregnant?

I have not met her parents, at least not yet. Maybe I never will. Do they have to know that I exist when they never wanted me in the first place?

Paul can now sit upright! I can hardly believe it. The Lama tells me that he has fully recovered from the fall. But his legs remain paralyzed and he cannot move them unless they get rehabilitated. Lama is a Tibetan word that means "happiness." His bruises still hurt and he advised us that we need to stay at least two days in the cave so Paul could recover. He is now working with acupuncture, endemic medicinal plants and a special combination of vitamins and minerals. Jag's brother stores everything in a backpack.

Paul gives me a kiss and a careful embrace. He is still pained with every move.

He was afraid that I would panic.

"I heard a strange sound. I was startled and when I looked around, I lost my balance. At first I slid down the slope but

Ben Bouter

then I clapped hard on a rock. My legs were numb and I did not have the strength to climb back up. The Lama heard my scream and he ran as fast as he could to help me. He is a masterful man!

I admire his courage.

"I can live without my legs," he boldly stated. "But not without you or Eva."

My belly is now noticeable. I need to get out of the house. But where will I go? I will go to my aunt, my dear aunt.

I show the Lama my father's replica. He laughs at the doll and he tells me that I cannot leave him in the cave. We will bury him together tomorrow. We will bury him ten meters away from the cave. He will help me.

Thus the story unfolds. Farhad's mother helped her. That must be the reason why he came looking for me. That was why he said that he knew a lot about me. So sweet!

I am now seven months pregnant. I do not want to be a burden to my aunt. She has quarreled with my parents. I need to go somewhere else where no one will find me.

Paul eats for the first time. I do not know what the Lama prepared, but it tastes good. There is a small burlap of herbs in the corner. There are small pouches of various plants from the Himalayas and other parts of India. It struck me that when I squatted in a hole in the monastery that the monks' excrement has the same color and mixture.

Night falls. There are plenty of blankets and I creep close to Paul.

"Darling, please. You move too much in your sleep."
He's right. I need to be patient.

I leave with father and the Lama the next day. The sky is clear and I have adjusted to the altitude. There is unusual silence in the mountains. It is an ideal place for contemplation. The Lama walks beside me. He hums to himself. We walk slowly. Life begins here in these mountains. He point to a light blue snake that moves through the fertile soil. The Indus, Ganges, Brahmaputra and majority of Asian rivers originate in the Himalayas. Without the mountain ranges, there would be no drinking water, no fishes, no grain and no life. The seemingly silent and lifeless mountain is the source of great energy. He is trying to explain to me the power of silence. He gives color as another example. White diffuses into a limitless array of bright shades. He teaches a lot with gestures and silence.

We stop at a red-painted pole.
"This is the place. Here he is not alone."
"I prefer to bury father in his own grave." I refuse his offer.
"This is his grave, besides hers. This is where it should be."
The Lama tells me.

I feel dizzy when I arrive in Ladakh. I am not used to the high altitude. I ask where the hotel is, because it appears to be a large complex. The clerk tells me: Drink a lot, even at night. You're not used to the altitude.

I stay in the hotel for three days. The people here are friendly. There are many shops and stalls on the main street. They sell clothes, pearls, fruits and vegetables. I feel at home with this place.

I will leave for the mountains tomorrow along with a group of foreigners. We will ride two jeeps.

I ask the driver if he can take us a little further because the dirty smoke is not good for my baby. He turns to me and apologizes immediately. We drive through barren plains. I see herds of yak accompanied by sheep and some dogs. A man shoots a lagging beast with his sling and he hits the animal's leg with precision. The beast rushes to join the herd.

We intend to visit two monasteries today. I find it weird that I was born in New Delhi but I have never been to a Buddhist monastery. My parents are not religious.

We are going up the Himalayas today. It has a famous monastery with great scholars. A few hundred meters below the monastery is a place for women. I'm curious about the place.

I could stay here. It is no longer reasonable to go back, although it is risky to have a baby in this circumstance. My body is not used to the pressure and the thin air. I have to drink a lot so I will not get dehydrated by the weather. I find it hard, but I drink even if I am not thirsty. I do it for the baby. I need to rest between two steps. I can hardly breathe; I think there is less oxygen here.

The women are nice to me. I can join them in a couple of weeks when I get past the monk's monastery. I will spend the night there. I find the trip very exciting. The baby kicks constantly.

We rest in the monastery. We have just arrived. My girlfriend has a backpack full of food and drinks. It's beautiful here. I have a new life here with my baby.

The monks use this cave to meditate. It is a luxurious cave, I understand. Most of the caves are much smaller. I do not know if anyone has been here. My friend points to a rope that I overlooked. We sit above the snowline and the ground here is always white. I cannot contain my happiness. This place is so wonderful!

I have cramps in my stomach. I guess I am about to give birth! My baby wants to see the snow!

There is a large plateau above us. Mama's bones are underneath the red stick.

"We give the vultures meat from the dead. We give them life." The Lama explains.

I sit down on the floor. There is nothing but bones in her grave. Is this what happened to Mama? Did she die immediately die after childbirth in the hands of a Buddhist nun, her own friend?

The Lama nods and smiles.

"We cut the dead into small pieces that the vultures can carry away. Sometimes they eat the fresh meat out of our hands.

I shudder at the images I see. I would love to push them into the abyss.

"I know that all Westerners think that the dead should be locked in a chest, deep down in the ground where no light can penetrate. They think that it's a better idea. You prefer worms that eat your rotten body rather than feed impressive birds that hover over the perennial snow?"

We bury Dad next to Mom under the platform. We stay together for a while in this wonderful place. This is where my journey alone begins.

I don't feel good. I am afraid that I am not going to make it. Please take good care of my baby.

PART 3

EVE

27

Do you prefer to give birth at home or in the hospital?
Lalitha has not yet thought about it. I let her decide. I want
her to be comfortable with the delivery. Good for Li, Better
for Eve.
I prefer a home birth, we have all the space now that we
live in a beautiful building on Zeemanstraat in Rotterdam. We
not only have a ground floor but three floors! Li, I always
called her Li. She has her studio in the house while I have my
office on the ground floor. Eve will feel right at home. The
house exudes an atmosphere of love, vitality and beauty. Two
lives come here together, intertwined with the history of the
magnificent property. There is room for a new miracle. I do
not know if a child can recognize the room where she is born,
no one remembers something about their birth. But Eve was
formed much earlier and if the baby leaves a protected space,
I do not want her to see the cold, bright light of an operating
room in a hospital. I might not be an expert, but I would think
that a child would want to be born safe in his own home. You
want to move from one secure place to another, like when you
move out of your parents' house and make your own home.
But Li tells me that she can handle childbirth and I leave it to
her. We all need to relax.
"Have a happy family," Farhad said. "You've had enough
misery."

We sold my house and we pay a reasonable rent for the place. We are intensely happy.

All is well with Eve until now. She is growing, she constantly moves and she is healthy. Li was initially worried that the lack of oxygen in the Himalayas would have serious consequences for Eve but so far all the indications tells us that everything is all right. I'm positive that we will have a beautiful daughter. Eve has survived the cold and the high altitude. There was less oxygen, but the place was pure. The rugged mountains, the white silence sounds different with that air and altitude. She must have a dizzying view of the snow and she must have felt the silence like an unborn child can hear the music in her mother's womb.

Li is now emotionally stable now that she knows everything about her mother. She often envisions the cave in her sleep, not as a nightmare but as a wonderful dream. It is deeply rooted in her subconscious. In retrospect, I realize that we were so close to Mama even if she was somewhere far away. We slept in the same cave where she spent her last days. It's as if we could hear her breathing. It seems a strange coincidence that the daughter she fought so hard so she could live returned to the cave thirty years later with a baby in her womb. Her death and her sacrifice to the vultures gave way to Li's birth. It is an unbelievable journey. You can review it over and over again and you can still discover something new about the experience. Months later, a scent and a sound like the Indian food in the basement can trigger a memory, an emotion, and an experience. India is now integrated in our system; it has enriched my relationship with Li.

She is due in one or two weeks. The tricky part is how she can reach the stairs to her studio with her bulging belly. She still works everyday and she tirelessly paints children- boys and girls from the orphanage where she spent her early years. She gives them a second life with her paintings. She illustrates them not as wretches, but special and unique creatures that deserve a decent home.

She wants to go back to the orphanage in the future even if none of the volunteers recognize her. That was so long ago and the hospice now has younger employees from all over the world. They open the door to a wonderful future that awaits the children.

"Paul, someday when Eva is older, we will go back to the orphanage. I want to make each child happy and let them understand that life is meaningful. I want to volunteer for at least a year. They need to realize that life is beautiful and they are special, just like Miss Paardekoper saw me as a unique individual that makes a difference in the world. They need to know that someone cares for them."

We live on the first floor, it is a wonderful suite with a spacious living room. It is so majestic that I feel like I live in a castle. Li's studio is in the front area of the second floor. The studio has magnificent lighting and we have designated the back portion as our bedroom. Sometimes I sneak into her studio at night just to see her paint. She does not realize that she is painting herself with child that she creates in the canvas. She fills it with intense colors, reminiscent of her childhood years.

Our bedroom also has a new addition: Eve's cradle.

We have a lift from the ground floor to the second floor so I can go up the house easily. My legs are limp as a ragdoll's.

I can hardly stand on my own. I know that I can live well despite the handicap.

My practice is now better. People see me and they know that someone who has a tragic experience can emphatize with them. Perhaps it's true. I think that I am more emphatic and my words are more sincere.

Li has sold one of her bronze statues. It is a statue of a dog relaxing on his back while a little girl rests her head on the canine's neck while she sits on her knees. It is a sweet picture of innocence and friendship. Four cities have one or more of Li's paintings and Rotterdam might well be next.

Our trip to India together, our good and bad experiences made us stronger. We have come to know Mom amidst the challenges we faced. I am grateful for the experience and I am in no way resentful because it caused me my legs. I have shared so much with Li in such a short time. I have spent days and nights with the love of my life in a cave five thousand feet above sea level. We have given a dignified farewell to Mama. Li read her mother's diary and she was impressed that she slept on the very same spot where she was born. Li looked forward to a bright future with her own daughter even her mother was no longer with her. I cannot describe how much the experience has intertwined out lives.

We showed Dad Mom's pictures. He has not seen these pictures before. He recognized her from the painting that Miss Paardekoper made. He made the same gesture that he did with the previous painting; he stroked the face with a sweet look in his eyes. There was some sort of recognition; it could even be endearment. The past is the last memory to fade. I showed him photos of beautiful young women but he barely showed interest. This picture was different and it evoked something in him.

We take once again take pictures of the paintings and put it in his drawer. We do not know if he misses the statue that Li took, but he seems content with the photos. He can see it, caress it. Statue or photo, it makes no difference. Mom's real portrait now hangs in Li's studio. She is with us every day. I had seen the painting before, but after the experience with India, I appreciate it even more.

She was unaware that she was pregnant when she posed for the photo. She had no idea what was in store for her. She is so beautiful and full of life and it moves me every time I look at the painting. I even talk to her out loud. I do not care if Li thinks I'm crazy. I feel so much affection for the woman more than love I have for my parents. Thanks to her, I have Li.

Li wants to make another portrait of Mom after she gives birth. She is still polishing the idea in her head but it envisions Mom with a big belly on one side of the picture while you see Li as a child at the back. I think it's a wonderful idea: mother and daughter united in one image.

"Home," Li confirms. "I prefer to give birth at home. The home is a warm nest while a hospital is cold and clinical."

"Good choice," the midwife says. "I can be here in fifteen minutes. Besides, you do not have a medical condition that entails a hospital delivery. The baby is usually born at night and the obstetrician needs to be paged before you can give birth. You can deliver your baby in the comfort of your own home."

The midwife is a nice lady. We are young and inexperienced parents, but she has brought lots of children into the world. I want to make sure that there are no risks.

We were concerned that Li might have inherited her mom's post-partum condition. The nun who assisted her said that something went wrong when Li was born. A portion of the placenta was damaged and it caused severe hemorrhage that caused her death. With respect to Tibetan tradition, the pole was dyed red in memory of her demise.

She told us that the risk was not hereditary but she will consult a gynecologist to make sure.

Mama caught a glimpse of Li in the last few minutes of her life. She cradled Li in her hands and held her to her face even if Li was still covered in blood. This was the baby she had fought for- a girl. "Lalitha", she whispered as she laid down her newborn child between her breasts as her last breath escaped.

Jag's brother and the Lama put me on a stretcher. I need to be strong for Li, even if it hurts a lot. My ribs are badly bruised and every move is unbearable. The Lama sees my face twisted in pain and gives me a quick drink that makes me drowsy. I make the trip down the mountain. Li is behind us. We often stop so she can rest. I do not want her lagging far behind.

"This is your father's grave, next to hers." The Lama told Li.

Everyone in the convent knows of the incident of Li's birth and her mother's death. The nun wrote it down for no one else but Li.

They made sure that Li was safe in New Delhi. They kept her away from the dangers of the streets. Everything is written in her diary but we cannot read it. It is written in Tibetan and Jag's brother graciously translated it for us.

The Himalayan vultures hover above my head. They float effortlessly while Dad floats with them. Death eventually gives way to life.

We stop once again. Li points to her belly. She is trying to tell me that Eva is in pain. She gasps. The oxygen is not enough. But the air gets richer as we make our descent. She is now standing beside me, I look at her. The three of us drink plenty of water. We have to keep ourselves hydrated in this altitude.

Why was I unaware that he was a married man?

She wrote in her diary. The man had not told her that he was already committed. His silence gave Li's life, but it killed Mom.

He is a charming Dutchman with black hair and a black mustache. He was with an archaeologist. There was no indication that she was his wife.

She had entrusted the nun with her diary.

The man who despised his child, who cheated on his wife with a gorgeous young woman was Li's biological father. We cannot ask him why he did it. We will never know his reaction if he knew that Li was his own flesh and blood, the daughter of his great love. But now I understand why he came home heartbroken after his second trip to India. He must have discovered that his true love was dead. He was divorced; he can take her to The Netherlands without him knowing that she was Li's mother. He knew nothing of the pregnancy, the birth and the child. They only told him that she died in the Himalayas and he could not reclaim her.

The vultures have devoured her. The nun was silent.

28

I call the midwife. Li is certain: contractions for a long time. She is panting and she has learned how to do pregnancy gymnastics in bead with coils underneath.

I echo the midwife's question: "How often do they come?" I ask Li.

"Every six minutes," Li replies.

Li is strong and I need to be strong as well.

"Try to get some sleep. It will take a long time before you deliver your baby. Call me after an hour if the contractions are between three or four minutes. Okay?" the midwife tells me.

"Fine," I reply.

"See you later then," she quips as she ends the call.

I put a cool washcloth on Li's forehead and I try to take a nap in an easy chair.

"Eve! I wonder what she will look like. You can't tell when she's still tiny, but who will she look like when she grows up?

"Mama did not have an obstetrician, Paul." Li says. "Was I born during the night? Did she die that night? I cannot get her out of my mind."

I feel the same. I imagine Li's mother struggling for her dear life. She ran away from home to escape the people who wanted to kill her child and she thought that her child would be safe on the Himalayas. Did they count the intervals between her contractions?

"Paul, do you believe in life after death? We never talked about it. Did you see the vultures on our way back? I found is strange that they hovered above us like they were guiding us." Li thought out loud.

I caress her soft cheeks. What can I tell her?

Children are vulnerable, malleable. I think it is gift that we are allowed to mold, to laugh and do crazy things with them. I often see children who are emotionally neglected in my practice. They are ignored and they often live a desolate life. I see children who are spoiled rotten, with no sense of discipline. But I am not yet a parent and I will do all that I can to be there when my children are sick or anytime when they need me. I will be an exemplary parent.

Li has a different background and we can complement and augment each other as needed. She is an incredible woman.

I still see her in my clinic, but she has changed. She now has a stronger personality and she is confident as she is charming.

She hated her father and it bothered her. She needed to get rid of all the anger, and that is why she came to me.

I felt overwhelmed with her presence. Not that I had feelings for her right away but she fascinated me. She was a dear colleague to me. Later I understood the crucial role that Eva Paardekoper played in her life. She was an erudite personality; someone who gives you reason to live and someone who inspires you. Li unconsciously emulated her; she was a kindred spirit. Thanks to her and Li's power and insight, and she made a new start at Baarnsch Lyceum. She decided to be a little Eva Paardekoper, that was her salvation. She looked up to her and she overcame the bullies. I admire Li a lot. She is emotionally stronger than me.

I had the idea of Li painting her father because she loved art and they both had a strong personality. I knew she could make the painting. She knew that others would think that she might be crazy, but she was willing to give it a try. It was an experiment for her and for me as well. I asked a colleague for his opinion because I had doubts but it turned out well. She even decided to go hiking with the doll. I would have discouraged her, but she was so motivated that I had to support her. The doll took her father's place and hatred disappeared. She loves her father! She has completely forgiven him. Compassion has pushed hatred aside.

When I was convinced that the therapy was successful, I realized that my job as her therapist was over. I felt a void. The caterpillar was now a happy butterfly that fluttered away from me and into a new world. I will never see that woman and she will vanish from my life like a pearl from a newly opened oyster that has slipped back to sea. I realized that I loved her after out visit at the nursing home.

It was wrong to sleep with that night. I was still her therapist and I had sex with my client. I was ashamed of what I had done and I did not contact her for a few months. I knew I had crossed the line and for that, she could sue me.

I dragged myself into her studio. She needed to see a therapist once again. Maybe she was going to sue me and I would plead guilty because of what I had done. But it was a ruse, Li was pregnant and she was in love me. Love was actually not the right word to describe what we felt for each other, it was more of affection, a deep friendship. I have never felt such a strong emotion. I had girlfriends in the past- I kissed, dated but that was only infatuation. A few weeks later and the sparks were gone. There was nothing else that could captivate the other. With Li, it was something else.

She told me that the contractions came within three minutes at the last hour.

I call the midwife. She says that she's on her way. I record the date and time in my diary: 11 P.M. May 14, 1996.

The midwife announces that she is three centimeters dilated. "That's nice. Labor has begun, but the delivery takes a couple of hours. An inch per hour is normal, but it's a case-to-case basis. You need to relax between the contractions. That way your body can produce extra endorphins that will reduce the pain. Did you know that? Remember to breathe when you get contractions, eh?"

Li nods. This is a new experience for her.

"You have to push after each contraction. That will ease the baby further into the birth canal."

She goes off once again. She needs to assist a client who is about to deliver her second child. The delivery will be easy. She is busy all throughout the night.

I sit next to Li and hold her hand. Women are special creatures, they fill their bellies with new life, and they are mothers from their first breath. I am also a father as I contributed a tissue or two with Eve. Children can be conceived through a seed, a post or even a tube, but a woman carries a new being with her and shelters it with warmth and care.

Tears slide down her light brown cheeks and make its way to her neck. She brushes them away with her hand. Beside her is Mama's diary.

The contractions really hurt. But I do not cry with something this big.

Ben Bouter

I put my cheek against hers. Words now pollute the air.
We both fall asleep.
I am awakened by my own snore. Li is puffing, she is in
intense pain.
"Should I call her back?"
It is five o' clock in the morning. Half an inch per hour, six
plus three is nine.
She nods. She moves out of bed every now and then. She
puts her hands on the back of the chair as the contractions
escalate. The midwife said that she needs to find a comfortable
position to ease the pain.
"Come quick."
"I'm coming. A healthy baby boy was just born. I will be
there in half an hour."
A few moments and you're a mommy, Li. And I will be a
Dad.
"I'm thirsty," she says.
"I'll get you a drink." I get up. She gives me a kiss.
"I'm a bit reluctant, but we can do it together eh, Paul?"
I see her as the girl in a few of her paintings. She dances,
laughs and plays a role like that children in the orphanage.
I see the same eyes, the vitality and vulnerability. It is an
amazing philosophical view when she is only three years old.

The midwife enters the room with a cheerful mood.
"Are you okay? It's hard, huh? I will just wash my hands
and then we'll see how far you are."
She disappears into the bathroom.
"You have a pretty place. A nice place to deliver a baby.
Let's see."

She reaches in. We look at her to see if the baby is on its way.

"Six inches! We're close. Do your best and in two hours you will give birth. Call me if you think that the contractions are closer to each other. You can scream if it helps you push. If the noise bothers you then you can scream into a pillow. It will help relieve the pain."

She rides into the night once again. I wave her off.

"Get yourself some sleep. You need to rest." Li implores.

"Well, I will stay here beside you. I can sleep in the chair. Do you like something to drink?"

The contractions come every four minutes with a one minute interval.

"It feels like a writhing pain in a huge belly." Li describes her ordeal.

I know the feeling. My family has a history of colon cancer and I had to undergo a colonoscopy where a small camera is inserted in your anus to check your intestines. I had to swallow laxatives the day before the exam so my guts would be empty. I writhed in the couch with pain. I had to squirm in pain for half an hour. Li was already in labor for seven hours.

"I'm not crying," Li consoles herself. "I am not crying with something this major. I will certainly not scream. Mama did not and I will not."

I kiss her softly on her dry mouth.

"Shall I rub your lips with cocoa butter?"

"Please! And lay a cold washcloth on my forehead, too." She implored.

I am glad that I can do something to help her. I get the potty as well.

"How long was Mama in labor?"

"It was long, at least all night. I do not exactly know how many hours."

"She said it was longer than twelve hours," Li said.

"She must be in intense pain otherwise she would not say that she is not crying over something this big. Why Paul? Why did her parents despise her? Why did she die?"

I know exactly what to say when I am with my patients. But with Li, I can only do so much as to hold her hand.

I doze off yet again. Li is catching her breath. I look at my watch: eight hours of labor. The midwife will be here soon. Just then, the doorbell rings and I walk towards the door. She walks up the stairs with an energetic bounce. She looks fresh with a different outfit.

"You only need an inch," she said a moment later. "Good. I'm staying!"

29

The water bag broke, it goes without saying.

I admire Li. She does not scream, she does not complain and she undergoes labor with patience. She endures everything for something big. We talk, laugh and look forward to seeing Eve, who remains hidden in her mother's womb. Is Eve as curious as we are with her? Does she understand that something special is about to happen? I'd really like to know what she thinks and how she feels. A baby feels her mother's mood. She listens to her mother's voice, undergoes her grief and joy.

"Paul, I am so excited! What did she get from me, you, dad and mom? I think that she looks just like us. I cannot imagine a better day. She is not an image made of bronze or clay, but a sculpture that we created."

The contractions are intense and in rapid succession. She has no time to relax. There are beads of sweat on her forehead. The only thing that gives her relief is the cold washcloth. What can I do?

Eve's head is now pressed on the cervix.

"We need to get ten inches. Are you okay?"

She smiles. My dear Li smiles. What did her mother look like when she was about to give birth? What did the nun do?

I feel tired and dizzy as I struggle to recall the moment. I want to ask her something as a distraction but I do not think that it is appropriate. I feel a twinge in my legs for the first time: phantom pain.

Why is delivery so difficult? Why must a person suffer so much in order to bring out something wonderful?

I remember her mother smiled when she saw that the monks gave her the privilege to join the monastery.

A new person comes from me, with marks from him, from me and her own.

She was in the enchanting coldness of the Himalayas. She must been a special woman! And the nun who had never experienced childbirth had expertly cut the umbilical cord of the newborn infant. I am shocked at the realization. Was her lack of experience the cause of the woman's death? There were no midwives nearby and there was only a nun who has never felt a man's hand. Love cannot compensate for ignorance. You are worse off with a bumpkin expert than with the hands of a well-intentioned volunteer. I believe that was the reason why the nun kept the diary. Was it a way for her to exonerate herself? Why was Mom in a monastery instead of a hospital in the valley?

I want to embrace Li and perhaps take away some of the pain. But the only weapon I have is that stupid washcloth that I hoped could take away her suffering.

The midwife knows what she is doing, she is well-experienced and we are assured that nothing will go wrong. The nastiest but the best part is about to come. Li gets contractions. I cannot even hear the word contractions amidst her ordeal. Woe to her! Woe to me! I sit here with crippled legs and I would anything to ensure Li's health.

The contractions are now thirty seconds apart.

"You are now on the second stage of labor," the midwife informs us.

She squeezes the vein in her head. She farts and poop comes out. She laughs.

"Do you still think I am all right?"

"That's quite normal," the midwife assures her. "The baby's head clears your bowels. Everything is fine."

I get restless. After ten minutes Li tells me that she does not feel any contractions.

"You have to feel like you want to take a shit, but with your womb."

"No, I can't do it."

"Feel the urge and then push."

"Yeah, but it's not much."

"Just watch me. If you have a slight urge to push, we're going to squeeze together. The child wants to get out, but we do not need to hurry."

The ways she says it alarms me. I know those phrases. The words are reassuring, but her tone is not.

"Squeeze your husband's hand so will have more power when you push."

I put my hand in hers. My arms have become strong these past months. We're going to make it together, Li. I do not say anything. I pat her cheek instead. I have to say something.

"I am so proud of you!"

"Can I squeeze his nose?"

"I cannot do it, I am tired." Li is drained from the arduous labor.

I see that she is exhausted and it has slowed down her contractions.

"The nun," I speak with caution. "Remember the nun, Li?"

Ben Bouter

I feel tears in my eyes. What can I say to her? But it must, we must.

"The nun said that Mom could not, remember? She was tired, and she had no strength. But the nun told her that if a plant can break through concrete, then so can you."

I burst into tears. It is so unfair. I sit here, I feel so helpless.

She strokes my head until the next contraction saps her of energy.

"Come on," the midwife tells her. "Come on! We have to keep going. We're almost there! I can already see her face!"

I do not know if what she is saying is true but a man has a goal, an endpoint. And that end point is Eve, her tiny head and her little body.

Li pushes with renewed vigor. Her body is under extreme stress. I am afraid that she will get a stroke with so much pressure on her head. Spit falls from her mouth.

"We're almost there."

A plant can break through the concrete; I say the mantra to myself. I repeat it over and over. Li's will is broken. Where else can she get power to continue?

A plant can break through concrete ... a plant can break through concrete ... a plant can break through concrete.

A plant has a purpose, does it have a will? Can it give Mommy new energy? She needs to be as strong as her mother. It's all so unfair. If sex is fine, then why is the denouement such a punishment? Who came up with that crap?

Li looks at me.

"You are stronger than a plant. You can do it, honey. Eve needs us. She needs you to push her out."

I abhor myself for such hollow and cowardly acts.

Her veins bulge with the stress. She squeezes my hand in half. Poop leaves her anus. But I see it! I see Eve's little blond head.

"I see her darling; she has a lot of hair. She got my hair, but her body is yours. She's lucky! She has the body of a goddess!" Eve is coming. Our child is coming, but not quite. She squeezes my hand and I squeeze back.

"Perseverance," she now continues with vigor, "It should come out now! Come on, push! Yes, yes, that's it. Keep going. Come on Miss Backs, she is almost out!"

Eva pops out her head. The midwife expertly handles the head and skillfully pulls her further. There is cream-colored grease in her spine. She looks all wrinkled, like a child who has been swimming too long in hot water. She cries! She is alive! There is blood in her head.

The midwife puts our newborn daughter on Li's belly. She puts her at a good distance so she can see Eve well.

"Paul she is such a beauty! Mom should have seen her!" We cry, for something this big.

The umbilical cord has been cut, and the midwife makes sure that the baby is immediately weighed and all her vitals are in check. She needs to make sure that everything is all right with the baby. It is now established, she is a healthy, baby girl. I can now hold my daughter. Eve!

Mom, you are now a Granny! She had to go through a hard labor just so life would continue. I put the photo of the painting that Miss Paardekoper made on Li's bedside table to encourage her. I turn Eve's face towards the painting. Eve, this is your grandmother. Grandma, this is Eve.

It is not yet over for Li. The placenta needs to come out, the midwife tells us.

"It was on the edge," she says. "It was intact. It has to come out, otherwise we have a problem."

We are grateful that Eve is healthy. Li's belly will soon subside. She is exhausted, but nonetheless happy. I cannot help but cry when I look at Li and Eve as they were almost died before they could breathe independently.

"Shall I take a picture?" The midwife asks. "It's for my own archive. I take pictures of all the kids and the mothers I assisted."

She takes our picture three times.

"You will get a copy. And now another picture on the count of three."

Eve is in her crib for the first time. No one remembers the details of his own birth, I assume that the ordeal must be tough to a newborn child.

Welcome, dear little Eva. The three of us are going to have a fantastic time together. What an astounding coincidence that Li came into my office. These are the best moments of my life. She is a unique woman and we have a child born with so much love.

30

The midwife is frantic. I can see it in her eyes, as she silently checks Li's condition. There is something wrong with the placenta. Li is using lots and lots of blood. I run my hand along her cheek.

"Everything will be all right, honey."

There are a few words that can strike fear as the ones I said. You can say it differently, but the words mean the same thing. At this point, I am not a psychologist. I am a partner and a father.

She gives Li an injection. Vitamin K, it says on the label.

The placenta is not completely removed. Where have I heard it before?

Blood, lots of blood.

Walked back and there was blood on the snow. Red, white. The hovering Himalayan vultures.

They immediately call the doctor.

"You must hurry. There has been a serious post partum hemorrhage. I need to go to the hospital. Li needs to go to the hospital."

"In ten minutes a nurse will come and she will watch over the baby. We need to go to the hospital," the midwife tells me.

She stops the bleeding in Li's vagina with tampons. She empties her bladder through a tube.

Dear Li, mother of our beautiful figurine. The only thing that makes life worth living.

Eve: one who gives life. We chose her name.

We dress Li in a gown; there is no time for nice clothes. She takes Li to the elevator. I stand at the top of the stairs, speechless. I force myself not to look at Li.

She's bleeding, Li is bleeding. Serious post partum hemorrhage. She used the Latin term for "arousing suspicions."

I hear her mother's words and I am sure that she hears them.

I am not okay. I am afraid that I will not make it. Please take good care of my baby.

I am left with Eve.
She sleeps.

31

The sister's name is Van Loon.

"I am Sister Van Loon, I am a weird string bean," she says out loud.

She certainly looks like one. Her hair was unfashionably cut. It looked like dried seaweed on top of her head.

She is not married and I cannot imagine how she can take care of babies.

I am torn. I want to go to the hospital but I do not want to entrust my daughter to this woman.

She notices that I am in a wheelchair.

"Spinal cord injury?"

"No, I test them before I sell these things!"

"How did it happen?"

"I was in the mountains of the Himalayas and I feel ten feet below and crashed onto a rock."

"You went to the Himalayas? It's a nice place. Barren, silent, white. It is a beautiful spot for meditation. It has wonderful monasteries. I've been there a couple of times. Did you go through Tibet on the Indian or the Nepal side?"

She is energetic and two more point on my prejudice barometer and I will consider her "normal." My mistake, I am once again too swift to pass judgment. You have never been to the Himalayas.

She stands over the cradle and peers at the sleeping child.

I want to tell her to stay away from her, but instead, I burst into tears.

"It's all right, Mr. Adama."

"She's dead," I tell her. My dear wife is dying. I am not crazy. She is dying exactly the way her mother did. She died during childbirth in the Himalayas. She died in silence with a nun at her side and the impatient vultures in the sky. Why the hell is this happening?

She is silent.

"You can go to the hospital if you want. They are in Dijkzigt. Shall I call a cab? You are in no condition to drive. I saw your car when I came in."

I doubt her and she sees it.

"Sir, I know what you are thinking. You're a psychologist, right. I saw the sign next to your door. You think that you are insane if you let your child stay with me. I know I am weird but I have been working in this field for twenty years and I think that says a lot. You will see me more often in the next few weeks. Who knows? I might fail this time. But you have to give me a chance. If I were you, I would go to the hospital to be with your wife. She is in a critical situation."

"Suit yourself. I know the way to the hospital." I reply.

I am quiet inside the taxi. I see ghosts on the road. She's dying. I'm sure that she will die just like her mother. Why does she have to go? She wanted a child, this child. We fit together and we still have a lot to do and explore together. I have not called my mom and dad to tell them that they are already grandparents and now I call them and say that their son is now a father and Eve is a half-orphan.

I think about the funeral arrangements while I am in the cab. Does she want to be cremated or buried in the ground? I do not even know if she is insured. We're not married; we do not even have a cohabitation agreement. All we have is a kid. Should I ask my mother for help? Do they want me to live in order to ensure that my daughter and I can be together? There is plenty of room for Eve. Shall I call Eva Paardekoper? She has previously made a miracle, maybe she can make one now.

I feel guilty that I got Li pregnant. The overnight stay was her idea. She stepped out of the bathroom naked.

The morning rush is over. I see people engrossed in their shopping. It is ten past ten. Mothers with children and women with a pram are everywhere. I see Himalayan vultures.

I look for the sign "*gynecology*" in the hallway of the hospital. She might be there or could she be in the *emergency room* or *obstetrics*? I have no idea and I decide to ask the reception. My head is just above the ridiculously high counter.

"Under what surname was she admitted? Adama or Backs?" The woman behind the desk stands over the counter with her back turned to me. She kindly looks down on me.

"You tell me!"

I explain the situation. She looks at her computer screen.

"When was she brought in?"

"About half an hour ago."

"I cannot find anything under those names. Are you sure she was rushed to this hospital?"

No, try the Hospital of Istanbul. I quietly tell her what Sister Van Loon told me.

"I just told you she is here."

I am distraught. My wife is bleeding to death and I am sitting here in the hallway of the hospital as she makes a call. Is she calling the emergency room? I have no idea.

They bring in cakes! Someone is the department is celebrating his birthday. Hurray, hurray! She greets the boy next to her and she gives him three kisses. I can see it because I am far out back. I do not see anything else and I am afraid that she will forget my distress.

She leans forward.

"She is ok, but you can go to the gynecology department and wait there. Take the first elevator and go to the second floor, go down the hallway and take a right."

They dig the cake with a fork while I walk away. I think I finally see the sign obstetrics after ten minutes. It is on the first floor.

The elevator doors open. There is a hospital bed with a tuft of hair on the pillow, the rest is covered with a white sheet. It is not Li's hair.

I press the button for the second floor. The lift stops on the first floor.

A man with a boy about I guess, five years old enters. He has black hair and dark eyes like a gypsy child.

"I have a new baby sitter," he declares. Then he notices me and asks: "What happened to your leg?"

I laugh. Children and adults are often curious with my condition.

"They are weak," I tell the boy.

"Paralyzed?"

"Yes, paralyzed."

"So you cannot play football?"

"I could not in any way."

"You can play tennis in a wheelchair."

"Yes, I can."
"Do you play tennis?"
"No, I do not."
I love these kids.

He has the eyes and the candor of Li when she was a little girl in India. She was happy because she could be creative with all the space. The volunteers at the orphanage saw her talent. She liked music, dance, drawing and painting. Discipline was taught with respect to time, but she was frequently free. When she arrived in The Netherlands with strict father and an absent mother, her creativity took on new forms. Li disappeared into her own world, full of dreams and ideas. Her imagination made her happy. She colored her own life with forms and ideas with hope because reality was stifling. Eva Paardekoper gave her back her space, her freedom. Nobody gave her as much as Eva did. She imagined everything and Eve encourage her to create it. She was there when Li needed her. Eva, I do not know a nicer name.

32

The elevator drops. We are back on the ground floor. I press 2 once again.

This time the lift goes straight to the designated floor.

I drive into the hallway. What did she say again? Hallway. But which way? I can turn either way. The sign above me tells me that I need to go left. I roll the chair as quickly as possible. I turn right and the end. What she said is true. The desk is empty; there is no one is sight. There is a space behind the counter, but I cannot see if someone is there. A nurse walks to the station.

"I've come for Lalitha Backs."

"Sir, that name means nothing to me. You should ask the reception."

"I saw her name at the reception."

"Wait, I will check."

Moments later, she asks me: "What's the name again?"

"Backs, Lalitha Backs. She's Ok, right?"

"Backs… Let's see… No, there is no Backs here."

"No, I said she is OK, she was brought here an hour ago because she was profusely bleeding after she gave birth."

"Ok, Ok. I will check. Did they tell you to wait here?"

"Yes, they told me to wait here."

"Well, that doesn't make sense. I will tell them that you are here."

"Hey, with Els... nice huh? Who? Yes, I was there!" She laughs. "But I have one question: is Miss Backs with you? Yes, please... Oh yeah, well... I will tell him... Yeah, bye."
"The doctor will be right out. You can wait inside the doctor's office if you want. It's the second door on the right."
"Is she dead?"
"What are you saying? I cannot tell you anything. The doctor will be here in ten minutes. They are still working."

I drive to the room. Another nurse opens the door for me and she smiles at me compassionately.
They are still working... with what? Are they trying to stop the bleeding? I want to scream at their secrecy and lack of information.
Of course, I understand. I get it. I need to calm down and not panic. Take a deep breath, Mr. Psychologist. Give yourself a moment. There are so many sick people in one day. So many emergencies, special cases and there are not enough nurses.

Inside the doctor's room, there are a few chairs along the wall and a table in the middle. There are old magazines on the small table. I brought along her mother's diary and I thought that it might help if read it to her. I look for an encouraging passage.

I cannot find my sculpture anywhere. Fortunately, I made a painting based on the original pience. It's so funny, I showed the picture to the admissions committee and everyone thought that it was original. The only difference is that my sculpture's pigtails are thinner than the real one. I am proud of myself.

I cannot believe it! I had browsed through the book but I have never read this before. She made a painting of the statue for crying out loud! The sculpture that her father had hidden in his drawer was made by Li's mother. She made it into a painting for her entrance exam. The museum wanted to pay for the statue. How much was it? Six Thousand Guilders or something. They had no idea.

Why did he take it? He must have stolen it. She certainly did not give it to her. She lost it, she missed it.

I have to tell Li that she saved her mother's statue. Did she know it and she did not tell me that Mama was a sculptor? How many times have I held the figure in my hand and I did not even have the inkling that she made with her own hands? We have an heirloom! My own Li is the daughter of a sculptor. I can barely contain my amazement that Eva Paardekoper, the colorful sculptor from Soest was her mentor and then this! Art Academy. It's amazing how things worked out. I have to tell her, it will keep her motivated. Perhaps Li has not considered that the statue is back in his father's cabinet. She will be a happy soul.

I see my little Eve at work in the studio alongside her mother. It cannot get more beautiful than that. The artful tradition is passed on from grandma to mother to daughter. Mama's perseverance will lead to new works of art. People will walk past it, but a few will look. Cute, niece, weird, stupid, brilliant. They have no idea that the work of art was made possible with sacrifice of a woman high in the mountains of India. I will put her in a pedestal. I will tell Li that Mama needs a place of honor in her studio.

I fear the knock on the door. The door opens in one fluid motion and a man in a white coat and a woman steps inside the room. They shake my hand. I cannot read anything from their blank expressions. White coat, white snow. I need to smile. White is good, it is beautiful. I see that the midwife is also here and she has white coat on as well. She gives me the pictures that she took of Li and Eve. Finally, I get my copy. They will get a special frame. Maybe it will inspire an idea for Li. A beautiful baby in the snow. That would be a wonderful idea! I already have plenty of idea for her new painting.

Ah Li, once you sculpt along with Eve the world will appreciate your sculptures and paintings. They do not know the value of art. We will give them a world of art- sculptures, monumental paintings, dance, and music. We'll do it together, Li. We are going to make everything better. Thanks to you, I gained a different perspective. Are you still in India? How long do we have to look at the yak before you can see my image? You tell me that you see a picture of Paul while on the other hand; I see a big, clunky side of the colossal animal's head and ass. I do not know. Do you have any idea? It must be something very elegant, something nice.

You are an artist from birth. The world is stunning, we have so many dreams. Maybe we can go back to the Himalayas with Eve so she can see the grandeur of the snowy mountains. It will surely inspire her. White is beautiful.

"Our team did everything we could, Mr. Adama."

You see? I knew it. They've done everything. Of course, what do you expect? It's their job, their task to heal people. That's what they're paid for. If her mother had such great help then Li would be here and she would be away from that weird family.

The nun was sweet. She did what she could, but she was alone. Your mother needed a team of experts. But you're here, Li and Eve is here. I am the happiest man in the world.

"The midwife made a wise decision to drive your wife to the hospital."

Yes, she had no children but she had a lot of experience in delivering babies. How many children and mothers did she take pictures for her archive? I have to check. I knew that she was an experienced midwife. Congratulations, Li. The future awaits. It's all worth it. We will have a wonderful time together with our daughter and a new life chapter begins with the three of us. Eve is waiting for us. She is watched over by Sister Van Loon. She is quite experienced as well; she has been caring for newborns for twenty years. You do not to worry. Everything is okay!

"But we're very sorry, we could not save you wife."

I stare at the diary. What did he say? Where am I?

"I can take you to her, Mr. Adama"

33

"Honey, stop for a while and get some rest." I tell Eve. "Do you remember who made that statue?"

"Grandma," she proudly replies as her pigtails merrily wave on her head.

Eve is putting the final touches on the image. You can see her pregnant mother upfront while Lizzie is evidently at her back. Well done! Two sculptors captured in one image. But before she finishes the painting, we add in some memories: two images and paintings that Li has made, including the boy with the snowball, her first boyfriend. I want to keep the image because Li's being is captured in the image. Eva Paardekoper made a cast from the statue of the girl with pigtails that came from India. It also goes into the collage. I also copied some of the paintings in Mom's diary and the painting of Li's mother. I also took a photo of Eva while she was in Li's belly. It is a monumental statue. I am so glad that Eva Paardekoper made it as a tribute to Li and Eve.

"Well done, Eve! You can do anything there for a pickle!"

The next day, a special truck transports the image to the center of Rotterdam. It is snowing.

CPSIA information can be obtained at www.ICGtesting.com
Printed in the USA
BVOW07s0750020115

381634BV00001B/94/P